Hugh Allen

THROUGH THE WALL

Illustrations by: Margaret Miller

AUSTIN MACAULEY™
PUBLISHERS LTD.

A CIP catalogue record for this title is available from the British Library.

ISBN 9781786292599 (Paperback)
ISBN 9781786292605 (Hardback)
ISBN 9781786292612 (E-Book)
www.austinmacauley.com

First Published (2017)
Austin Macauley Publishers Ltd.™
25 Canada Square
Canary Wharf
London
E14 5LQ

An Introduction

There have been two world wars, each of which lasted several years. This is the tale of Hans Bernauer who was born in Berlin, Germany a year before the outbreak of World War II. His parents were Jews and, at that time, Hitler was endeavouring to rid his country of all Jewish people. Hans survives the war and then finds himself facing life under a frightening communist regime.

The story opens, however, with an aerial battle scene that took place over the Somme in 1918 during the First World War. The dogfight is between British Sopwith Camel biplanes and German Fokker Triplanes. One of these becomes significant to the main story.

Within the main story is woven an adventure of an English boy who gets caught up in a dangerous international situation.

So it is a tale of war, of hardship, and of hopes for a better life to come. Will Hans realise his dream, and what has this English boy to do with it anyway? Read his story…

Chapter One

Aerial Battle Over The Somme 1918

The First World War: 1918

Allan McNab Denovan is lost in action over the Somme battlefields.

Aircraft: Sopwith Single Seater SE5A B511

"The clouds were scudding across the wide-open expanse of sky. The air smelt fresh. The wind was strong, though not wild enough to prevent take off. Allan McNab Denovan looked across to his Sopwith Single Seater and then, again, looked up into the sky.

The aeroplane stood ready, and rocked a little with the buffeting air. Allan was prepared, too, fully kitted and slightly uneasy at the prospect of an aerial battle. It was 1918, in the springtime and in France. Late March, the 26th, could be wonderful with the promise of warmer weather coming. Allan felt little of the hope of summer because this was the battle zone of the Somme. Sometimes he felt privileged to fly. He wasn't having to survive the trench warfare, with its inhuman miseries of gas, bomb, machine gun, and sodden underground hideouts. He wasn't facing a new day of offensives: of being ordered out of the trench and running headlong into German gunfire. The list of the names of the dead and lost grew ever longer. The shadow of this took away any potential thrill of flying.

He stubbed out his cigarette and ground it into the path. He sighed deeply, took a breath, and walked over to the Sopwith. The mechanics had checked it over, as they had with the other three. Once strapped in, comfortable, and composed, he indicated to the airman on the ground to swing the propeller. She fired up immediately, but he stayed put to warm up and allow his flying companions to prepare.

They took off into the wind, one after the other, first bumping along the field and then having that replaced by the thrusting winds. Visibility was excellent. The clouds were not too much of a problem. They flew north over Arras, watching all the time for signs of enemy aircraft. The noise from the Sopwith engine drowned out most opportunity of hearing others. Good visibility and sharp eyesight were essential.

The first sign of trouble was the sharp rat-tat of a machine gun. Allan twisted round and caught a glimpse of a red triplane, but not far enough behind. The triplane bore down on him; it must have hurled itself through the patch of cloud.

'Oh God!' Allan spoke aloud, 'He's got it in for me.' The other three Sopwiths were turning to face their attackers. They were two Fokker triplanes which peeled apart. He could see the black cross and other symbols painted on the fuselage of his pursuer. He swung the joystick violently to hurl the plane out of the firing line, and pulled it back to force him into a steep climb. 'So far so good,' he thought, and prayed that his companions were safe.

His pursuer, unknown to him at that moment, was the Red Baron. This pilot's real name was Baron von Richthofen, and he had become a legend for his amazing flying skills. On this day in March, he took to the skies with another younger German pilot, Lieutenant Udet. Together they had been hunting the British, hoping to engage in a dogfight, flying and shooting to bring the enemy down. Were it a film, the scene over the extensive woodlands would have been pure adventure: two German Fokker triplanes swooping on to four British Sopwith biplanes.

The Red Baron picked his target and dived at it, with the machine gun chattering its deadly bullets. Allan climbed and then turned the Sopwith alongside again. Somehow, he must turn his attacker into the attacked, by getting behind him. He pushed the plane to its limits, its engine screaming at full throttle. He lost sight of the Fokker, but saw, with horror, one of the Sopwiths spewing flames from the engine cowling. It was going down, but he couldn't see the pilot. There was no time to assist, not with his own troubles. He forced the plane on round and suddenly plunged. The Red Baron remained in hot pursuit, and seemed to be gaining. He knew he was, and relished the thought of marking up another victory. As Allan tried to pull out of his dive and gain height, the Red Baron lunged at him from the side. His machine gun rattled and bullets tore into the Sopwith. There was a flash and the Sopwith spun out of control. Already close to the ground, and with flames spewing out, it skimmed the treetops, caught a taller one and landed tail up.

The Red Baron recorded his victory in his usual way. He asked his silversmith to make another miniature cup with victory no.69 inscribed on it. Lieutenant Udet, his flying companion, brought down the other Sopwith. The two remaining flew at full throttle back behind the safety of the allied forces.

There was no more flying activity that day, but the ground battles continued with the rattle of rifles and thud of exploding shells. The maiming and killing persisted on both sides."

It was time to go out, so I put the book on the floor, upside down so it would stay open at the place.

Chapter Two

Kristallnacht 1938

Before the Second World War in Germany, Jewish families are broken up and many Jews disappear.

Hans never knew his mother or his father. They were taken from him when he was only two years old. At that time the city of Berlin was unsettled. It was before the Second World War and the Nazis were in power. For many, this was good. The new political party created work and hope, where before, poverty and hopelessness reigned. For some, the Jews, it was the beginning of the end.

Hans was born into a Jewish family. Jakob and Anna celebrated the birth of their first child by closing the shop early one day, and bringing their friends and neighbours in for a party. Downstairs, only the shop window was lit up. The lettering, gold-edged on the glass, read *J. Bernauer, Gold and Silversmith*. The shop was in Leipziger Strasse by the Potsdamer Platz, a fashionable area of expensive shops and restaurants. Noisy trams that screeched on the rails served the area alongside cumbersome double decker buses. It was busy in the daytime and again at night, when the cafes and restaurants attracted pedestrians. Passers-by could look at the display in the Bernauer's shop window and wonder, although many of the pieces of jewellery and expensive watches were locked in the safe. Upstairs, in the flat, the lights were bright. With the windows open, bubbly conversation wafted out on the warm night air. Their baby, Hans, was sleeping through this, lying almost hidden beneath a patchwork quilt in his cradle. Now and then guests would peer at him, cooing with delight.

Two years later, the city had changed. Hans was a toddler, and the joy of Jakob and Anna. But now, any Jewish people were being treated with suspicion. The Nazi party encouraged this, and soon the Jews were shunned. Increasingly, they lost their jobs; their children were segregated at school. The mood gradually became darker.

One night, the situation became far worse. That night became known as Kristallnacht, and the date was November 9th, 1938. Gangs rampaged through the streets of Berlin, seeking out any Jewish shops and businesses.

Jakob and Anna had closed the shop, locked away the best as they always did. They recorded the day's takings and went upstairs to the warmth of their flat. Hans was playing with his toys and hadn't noticed Anna slip downstairs to help her husband. They had felt the change of mood in the city. And they had lost some of their regular customers. Often, over supper, they would talk of it with hope. "It's only a phase and it won't get any worse. We'll be alright, you'll see. The government will have to put a stop to all this nonsense."

In his heart, Jakob feared otherwise. To other Jewish businessmen he would say that he could smell the coming storm and see the dark clouds gathering. And the others would agree. He never quite knew whether they believed him or thought of him as an alarmist. For him though, the threat was real. He had prepared for the worst. That night was almost the worst.

Anna and Jakob finished their evening meal together. Hans, exhausted from his day, was asleep in the corner of the living room. Beneath his quilt, and wrapped in the love of his family, he dreamt of sunny days and the freedom to run through the woods by the big lakes, his favourite Sabbath times.

As they put down their knives and forks, they became aware of shouting outside, probably further along the road. This was interrupted by the sound of breaking glass and a large cheer. The noises came closer. Anna went to the window and drew back the curtain.

'Anna, come away from there. Come away.'

'What's going on, Jakob? What is the noise? Is it glass breaking? What do you think it is?'

'I don't know, but you take little Hans into the bedroom. Stay in there until I tell you.'

Anna opened her mouth to protest.

'Do as I say. You must.' As Jakob spoke these words, he was drowned out by the clamour in the street below. The crowd had now gathered outside their shop and from the rabble emerged a single chant: "Jew. Jew. Jew." The pace of the shouted chant grew, and it had menace in its sound. That though was shattered with a great crash and the echoing tinkle of glass splintering. He knew it was the shop window. He stood away from the upstairs window and held his breath. The chanting began again, and Jakob felt fear. He reached to the door and switched off the light. That provoked further uproar outside: "Jew, Jew, your light is going out!"

Someone shouted, drawing attention to another premises, another business about to be wrecked. The crowd moved noisily away to destroy another Jewish family's peace.

Jakob was badly shaken. He could feel the trembles. It was quite a few moments before he felt he could call to his wife using a steady voice.

'Anna, Anna come, come quickly.'

She came and they drew great comfort from one another. Together, they crept downstairs. All across the counter, strewn everywhere on the floor were shards of glass, slivers and glistening splinters. Together they stood in the doorway, not speaking but surveying the damage and wondering what the future held for them.

Anna glanced at the door to the street. She was going to speak but halted. Something had caught her attention. Pasted to the glass of the door was the Star of David. It was not put there as an honour, but to mark the shop as Jewish, thereby stopping custom – as if the damage wouldn't. Anna pointed to it and looked to see Jakob's reaction. He showed no response beyond his silent pondering.

Behind the silence of both of them was deep fear. This was not only for their business, so successfully built up from modest beginnings. Jakob was highly respected in the jewellery trade, and many important Berliners were his customers. Often they would commission particular pieces – a brooch, a tiara, earrings for special occasions. He knew he would lose much now. Jakob feared for Anna, and feared for little Hans.

He knew of the rumours of the arrest of Jewish people. These were never openly reported, but everyone had heard. Jakob was prepared, even though they were caught out by the events of Kristallnacht.

The two of them spent much time that night clearing up, and then covering the windows with boarding. Lastly, Jakob sent Anna up to see to Hans, and then to go to bed. "I'll be up soon," he said.

Moments later, he opened the safe and quickly pulled out its contents. They tumbled into a bag he held open. As he did so, he could almost see the gold, the diamonds and other gems, the money, too, even though each was in its own wrapping. He knew everything in his stock – its history, its maker, and its worth. He knew what he must do. The safe clicked shut and Jakob let himself out of the shop and into the street. He was carrying the bag.

Anna fell asleep through exhaustion. Jakob, when he returned, could not sleep. The events of the night troubled him as would an evil omen. At breakfast, it was only Hans who had enthusiasm for the new day. He barely noticed the strain in the household and the near silence of the meal. Jakob reached over the table and took Anna's hand.

'Anna, you must take Hans to Heinrich and Maria. I know they are not our family. But no Jewish family is safe now. Pack for him as much as you can carry. And, Anna, take these two packets. One is some money to help them care for Hans. The other give to Heinrich. He knows you might come.'

'Jakob, we cannot do this. We cannot give Hans even to friends. I won't do it.' Anna was angry, very angry and upset.

'Anna, we're living in dangerous times. Tell them it is for a week, but you must go.' Anna felt the strength in her husband's order, and she collapsed into tears. She left clutching Hans to herself.

That night, the gang returned and beat upon the door. Fearing more damage, Jakob went down and released the catches. As the door of the shop swung open, a torch shone into his face. "Get him. Get the Jew," came the order. Jakob was grabbed, dragged roughly into the street, and taken away.

Two days later, they came for Anna. She was packing the last pieces before leaving. She was too late.

Chapter Three

Life at the Schmidts'

Hans cried for nearly three weeks. He was a toddler and two years old. He was used to the confines of the flat over the shop. Even though the flat had space, Hans was free to run and play wherever he liked. Anna, his mother, was never far away. When she was busy in the shop, the door to the stairs was open. She could hear him. Sometimes it was the quiet that troubled her. She wondered what he was doing!

Here, living at 13 Stallupöner Allee, he was lonely and felt utterly lost. Heinrich and Maria were kind. They had given him his own room. From the window, he could see into the garden and over to the woods beyond. That was frightening. The distant woods were dark and quiet at night. From the flat, Hans could always see streetlights and often hear people walking by and chattering. Night-time with the Schmidt's was silent. Hans found some comfort as he lay in his strange bed. Maria would play the piano downstairs, and the music led Hans into other worlds.

Each morning, Heinrich Schmidt would read the paper at breakfast. Then, dressed smartly in a suit, he would go by car to work. Hans wondered why he couldn't work at home. Heinrich was an inspector in the post office. He worked with engineers on telephone systems, checking the systems and arranging new tasks. Mostly he worked at a desk in his office. Sometimes he joined the men on a job, especially on sunny days.

Heinrich would have been in the army or maybe in the air-force or navy. With his endless interest in military aeroplanes and air battles he would have chosen the air-force, the Luftwaffe. All young men had to join up. That rule had been in force since 1935, when he was twenty-five years old. For him, it was not to be. His job in the post office was to maintain good telephone communications in and out of Berlin. His expertise and knowledge were too important and so he remained behind. Nearly all his friends had joined one of the three forces. He heard from them occasionally. Some were having a good time and had been posted to interesting places. Others felt out of place in uniform and longed to be released.

Heinrich was not a Jew. He had known Anna, Hans's mother, from school days. When Anna married Jakob, Heinrich went to the wedding. They remained firm friends. Heinrich and Maria spent many happy hours with Jakob and Anna Bernauer, visiting the Olympic Stadium to watch athletics, walking by the Havel Lakes, or window shopping along the Kurfurstendam on a Sunday. So they gladly took in Hans, maybe for a week or two. Heinrich suspected that it could be for much longer.

He could feel bad times coming. Already Jewish families were either escaping out of Germany or were disappearing, as did the Bernauers. Hitler was in power and he was stretching the boundaries of the Third Reich. Heinrich felt he could do little. He was fearful of speaking out in support of Jewish inhabitants. He feared for his and Maria's safety. They had no children of their own, but now had to care for this Jewish child. They had no official papers for him. How long could they conceal him for? Was it possible to obtain adoption papers? Could they get papers for Hans that did not mark him as a Jew? Heinrich pondered these issues. He shared his concern with Maria one breakfast time.

They decided that they should try to find a way of obtaining forged documents, copies of the official ones, though with Hans's name on them. They would pay whatever was necessary. First, though, they would wait for two weeks to have word back from Anna or Jakob. No word ever came. It was after the war that they discovered that both Anna and Jakob had perished in Auschwitz. Their crime against the state was to be Jewish. They were exterminated in the gas chambers of the evil concentration camps.

Hans gradually settled, and accepted the love and attention given to him by Maria. Sometimes he would sit on her knee at the piano and fascinate himself with the sounds he could make. Bashing the keys was frowned upon, but otherwise he could experiment. A year later, they found a retired music teacher who would come each week to teach Hans to play. Hans was gifted, they decided.

He was free to roam the house; the garden, too, when the weather was fair. His few toys remained in his bedroom and he preferred that. He felt safe in there with his own possessions and a photo of his parents on the locker by his bed. The Schmidt's would occasionally bring him a new book to look at, or one full of stories that Maria would read to him at bedtime. Those were treasured moments.

The kitchen was his favourite room downstairs. It was the one room where something happened. The other rooms seemed to be where grown-ups would talk, maybe over a meal, maybe with a pot of coffee and a plate of cakes. But in the kitchen he could watch Maria bake and sometimes, when she was not in a hurry; he could stand on a chair and help. Maria called him her useful hindrance.

There was one place in the hallway that remained a mystery to Hans. It was the door near to the front door. Hans never saw it open and never asked what was through it. It led to the cellar steps. Heinrich used the cellar as a workshop. It was the place he felt most relaxed because he could pursue his hobby which he had had since his own childhood. He was fascinated by aeroplanes and, in particular, military planes from their earliest times.

He made models of them, not from kits but from anything he could find that was suitable. He had built a Sopwith Camel biplane. It was of the type used in the First World War. Normally he painted each model accurately and put on the correct markings. Alongside each model was a written note of that aeroplane's history. He had written more than a brief note about this Sopwith. The story of it had interested him more than the others. And the reason was that it had been engaged in an aerial battle in the skies over France. Heinrich had researched the history of various World War One aeroplanes, and this particular event stood out.

He learned that the pilot, Allan Denovan, had been flying in a group of four Sopwith Camels. He was shot down by the Red Baron. The Red Baron had an assistant on that day, and the two of them were flying Fokker triplanes. The assistant, Lieutenant Udet, later became a high-ranking officer in the Luftwaffe and he lived in Berlin. His house was now, all those years later, the very one in which the Schmidt's lived. Heinrich did not know this at that time.

The model Sopwith was painted red as a reminder that it had been a victim to the Red Baron. He sat back in his chair and looked at his model, pondering the markings he should put on the wings.

His mind wandered, and he thought anxiously about Anna and Jakob. Hans was a little more settled and seemed to enjoy some of his new life.

Together with Hans, Anna had brought an envelope for safe keeping. It contained, she explained, details of where Jakob would hide the shop's valuable collection of jewellery, and also the document proving ownership of the shop. Heinrich had the large brown envelope lying on the work bench. It would be safe enough for now, he thought. He leant forward to pick up his latest model again. As he did so, it occurred to him that he could roll up the envelope and slide it into the fuselage. He carefully removed the propeller and engine, leaving a hole into which this fitted. Once back together, it seemed no different and simply looked like a model alongside many others. He felt lighter now, as though a trouble had evaporated.

Maria called, so he tidied the bench and left the cellar. It was a world that Hans knew nothing of.

Chapter Four

At War with Britain 1939

As the days passed, Hans saw less and less of Heinrich. Maria lost her easy and friendly manner. It was as though she was worried. Day by day she fretted. At the kitchen table, she pored over bills and receipts. Friends came less often. Heinrich came home later, and generally left in the morning before Maria or Hans were up. Once or twice Hans was awake and slipped out of bed to find Heinrich. Heinrich would send him back to his bedroom, using firm and almost unfriendly words. Hans gave up.

So he created his own world in his bedroom. He would become absorbed by his books. Maria had read them to him several times and he knew the stories. On the floor, he would create a town with wooden bricks and tin plate cars. One car was clockwork but no longer worked. He wished he could ask Heinrich to mend it.

At night he entered another world. In bed he talked with Freddy and Mitzi, the two teddy bears that had always been with him. He told them about the day, about events in the house, about Maria's cooking and her piano playing. He hummed them the tunes that he had learned from the old music teacher. He made up an imaginary room behind the mysterious door in the hall. He told them when he was frightened, and clung to them in thunderstorms. Hans was not aware of the other storms brewing. The clouds of war were gathering all over Europe.

Heinrich followed the political scene each day by reading the paper and listening to the wireless. The news from his point of view was very discouraging. The Jewish people continued to be hounded from their homes and their work. And the Third Reich, the newly formed Nazi party, was flexing its military muscles. On 12th March 1938, Hitler ordered the invasion of Austria.

Within a day, Austria had become part of the Reich and not a shot was fired. The next year, was declared against Czechoslovakia. Poland was invaded in September the same year.

After failed diplomatic pleas, Britain and France were prompted to act. War was declared against Germany. Now the Western world was drawn into conflict again, so soon after World War One. Dark clouds continued to blot out the blue skies and any hope of peace.

Heinrich secretly feared that worse was to come. He felt that the aggression of his country would provoke an even wider war, maybe with the United States of America as well. He voiced these fears to Maria one day, when outside the rain was torrential. The garden was awash. Nobody ventured out on to the street. For a Sunday afternoon, that was most unusual. Maria suggested that it was more than the rain that people feared. Hans was in his room, engrossed in building a wooden brick cottage with room for his toy soldiers to take shelter within.

"Heinrich, we cannot stay here and mutter about the dark clouds. What can we do?" Maria leant over the table and took his hand. Their coffee was left unfinished.

"My work is here. They will not let me join up."

Maria nearly smiled but would not allow it to show. For her, she was pleased. They were together and safe, for now. She knew Heinrich sometimes longed for action, and she watched him become more agitated week by week.

"I work every day putting in new lines for telephones in government offices. I have to have each one checked for security. Nobody is civil anymore, and I seem to be dealing with bullies. Some of the Nazi officers are the worst. It is hard to work with that oppression. And, Maria, I fear for you and little Hans. He is three now, and like a son to us. If ever..."

Maria broke in, "No, don't say that, Heinrich. We will always be together."

"But if they find out about Hans being a Jew, we will be arrested for hiding him."

"Hans has the right Pass, and on it he is not Jewish. We have adopted him. Never even say the word Jew; it is too dangerous." Maria looked intently into Heinrich's eyes. She could see how troubled he was.

Then he spoke. "Maria, let's make our cellar a safe place. The door locks and down there we can store our best things, and even hide there if..."

So the workshop tools were cleared away. Together with the model aeroplanes, they were put into the attic. All except one. Heinrich kept out his latest model, the Sopwith Camel. That was tucked under the bench before being surrounded by boxes of pictures, of books and china. They brought photo albums down there, too, so the family and their friends would be remembered. In the middle of the large underground room they put some comfortable chairs and stored food and bottles of drink. After that, they felt better, except they realised that little Hans knew nothing of the cellar room. They brought him down from his bedroom. Heinrich picked him up and carried him down to the hall. They told him about the stairs behind the door, and the room below. Hans was wide-eyed, partly afraid, and also excited to know, at last, this mystery.

As Heinrich turned the door handle, Hans became solemn and clung on tight. It was dark until Maria switched the lights on. How disappointing. It was a room with only one very high window. Filled with boxes, there was little space left. Definitely not a toy room and little to excite Hans. They returned to the kitchen and the cellar door was locked.

Chapter Five

The War Rages On

Heinrich often reflected on the news. All the time, day by day, on the wireless and in the papers he heard and read about the glorious Third Reich. Hitler had become a formidable warlord with utterly ruthless aides in his senior officers. The Gestapo struck fear, not only amongst enemy troops, but even at home here in Berlin. No-one spoke any words of criticism about the government. Nobody dared question the meagre rations each family received. Work places had become cruel and ill paid. The people of Berlin looked grey, and Heinrich wondered whether it was worse elsewhere. The news of glorious victory did not match his experience in 1943. The propaganda spoke endlessly of a glorious future for the people of Germany.

The discreet whispering on street corners was of disappearance. First it was the Jew, and this was continuing. But others vanished overnight. Arrests were commonplace but never spoken about. Fear increased and the Berliners felt insecure and unsafe. The golden future was, surely, a myth.

They had good cause to fear. The storm broke on 22nd November. Heinrich had returned home early. He brought with him a briefcase full of work which he intended to complete after supper.

There had already been over three hundred bombing raids. Parts of the city were rubble heaps where people scurried by or only stopped to salvage oddments. Fires burned on after the Allied bombers had begun their long, dangerous flights home. The suburb of Charlottenburg had survived well. Heinrich at least knew they had a good chance of remaining safe, for there was little industry in that part of the city to be targeted.

On that particular November day, cold and grey, the Allies launched a colossal bombing raid. Seven hundred and eighty bombers flew over in waves. The Berliners heard the air raid sirens and scurried to their shelters. Those who were already homeless hid amongst the rubble and sought out any remaining cellars for their safety. Following the mournful wail of the sirens came the first drone of aircraft. There were so many that the sky was darkened. Tonnes, hundreds of tonnes of bombs were dropped. There was barely time to recover from the shock of nearby explosions before the next onslaught began.

From their home in Stalluponer Allee they could hear too much, and had seen some of the enemy aircraft in the skies above. Heinrich had a compulsion to stand outside by the front gate and watch for the returning bombers. He assumed the targets were factories, railways, and bridges. Charlottenburg would be safe. The enemy would achieve nothing by bombing this quiet suburb. He returned to the house, where Maria was keeping Hans busy in his bedroom. They had spread out the bricks along the floor to make a track for his cars. He was racing them through the gaps, and he shrieked when one hit the end wall of the bedroom. Heinrich pushed open the door.

"Maria, bring Hans to see these aeroplanes. They are mostly Lancaster's. Come, I'll carry Hans." He was seven years old now, and was capturing some of Heinrich's enthusiasm.

"No, Heinrich, it's not safe. We should stay in. We should be in the cellar."

Heinrich persisted and explained that the bombs had already been dropped. The aircraft were already turning for home.

The three of them were by the front gate. Hans stood on the wall, clutching the iron railings. He felt excitement but touched with childhood fears of the unknown. He didn't know what to be afraid of, but sensed the tension in Maria.

"Look, look! They are coming closer!" Heinrich pointed. This group of four were coming in their direction. They stood there fascinated, although Maria clung to Heinrich and together they kept Hans close.

The aircraft droned overhead, gaining height. As Heinrich gazed up he saw a double movement. Something fell from one of them. He realised the meaning and was struck with terror. He choked on his words, which were lost as the whistling noise intensified. He caught up Hans and yelled to Maria to get into the house.

Before they could, there was an intense crash and, as they heard the explosion, they were caught up in it and were flung through the garden. The bombs had been dumped to save weight on the long flight home. One fell through the roof at the back of the house and the other at the end of the garden.

The house had erupted in flying debris and flames. The sky turned black and was filled with masonry and tiles being flung violently in all directions. Those moments were nightmare experiences for the three of them. Hans was sobbing and coughing the sandy soil from his mouth. Maria called for Heinrich with hardly any voice. There was no sound from Heinrich. Maria pushed her way through the rhododendron, feeling her limbs. Nothing seemed broken, but her body ached. Her eyes were clouded and she wiped them with the back of her hand, then noticed the blood. Somewhere on her head she was bleeding.

She stumbled over Hans, tripped, and fell. Hans whimpered and she drew him close.

"Heinrich, Heinrich, where are you?" she called. There was no answer.

The front gate creaked open and a voice called to Maria. It was the man from along the road. They were friendly and had met up sometimes. In no time he had found her and Hans. He brushed the grime and dust from each of them. Hans clung tightly to Maria. Maria looked about her, her face full of fear.

"Heinrich, we must find Heinrich."

"Come," said the neighbour, "my wife is there and she will take you to our house. I will find him."

"No, no, no, I cannot go." Maria was almost screaming.

The neighbour led her and Hans through the gate. He was firm and gentle to them. As he did so, he looked back to what had been their home. There was little left of any use. The roof and the upper walls were blown away in the bomb blast. The ground was littered with rubble, glass, and the remains of furniture. The house was devastated and, in his opinion, beyond repair.

Maria let herself be guided. The man's wife led her and Hans over the road and away from the black scene. Heinrich was found slumped in the shrubs. He was still, and the neighbour feared that he might he dead. Tentatively he pushed through and spoke. "Heinrich, can you hear me?" He bent down and touched him. Heinrich fell to one side and lay still.

By now many others from the street had gathered by the gate to stare at the devastation of the stray bombs. One man noticed the neighbour moving Heinrich. He clambered across the masonry and knelt down. He felt his face and took his wrist. There was warmth and there was a pulse. He was alive, but unconscious. Together the two men looked and felt for broken limbs. It seemed that Heinrich had no breaks but had been hit severely enough to knock him out. They decided to carry him away from the ruin to be with Maria. The crowd at the gate parted to let them through. No-one spoke. They stared at what had been a home only a short time before. They had seen other parts of Berlin shattered by bombing raids. This time, they realised, it could so very easily have been their own houses. That day, the Schmidt's lost theirs totally.

A doctor was called, and it wasn't long before Heinrich's eyes flickered and opened. Maria gasped with relief. He looked toward her, and then his eyes closed. The doctor explained to the three of them in the room what they must do for Heinrich, and to call him again if there were any alarming signs. He left. Hans crept into the room and ran across to Maria. She caught him up and together they watched the sleeping form.

They stayed there for two days. There was very little to be rescued from their home. Heavy rain had followed soon after the bombing raid, and was continuing this day too. Maria rescued a few mementos and two of Hans's toys. Of Freddy and Mitzi, his favourite companions in his bedroom, there was no sign. It was impossible to get into the cellar, if anything of it remained. Much of the house was in a dangerous and unstable state. The red aeroplane was buried beneath the tons of rubble. She did find some sodden blankets and carried them away to dry. When she arrived back at the neighbour's house, she found that Heinrich was well on the way to recovery. Already he was thinking of a plan for them and was becoming impatient. They agreed that the following morning they should leave.

Heinrich had kept in touch regularly with his ancient aunt. He felt sure that they could take up shelter there, for the time being anyway. She lived in Hufeland Strasse, in the middle of Berlin. It was nearly nine miles from Stallupöner Allee, a little to the east of the city centre. Aunt Giselle lived in a flat on the fifth floor. Heinrich assured Maria that they would be welcome, but he had an inner fear. They had been fortunate in Charlottenburg that it had not been bombed. At least, not until the stray bombs that week. He didn't know whether his aunt had received his message. He didn't know if that part of the city had been hit by Allied bombers. Would the block of flats be standing?

His aunt was so old-fashioned. Her home was full of ancient furniture, all heavy and dark. She could be an awkward person at times, and would refuse to be helpful or friendly. Heinrich called her his Prickly Crab. He had only visited her a few times, mainly out of a sense of duty. So the three of them set off across the city with a sense of unease about their destination.

There was very little traffic in the streets. Around them, as they reached the centre, they saw more and more devastation. Some parts of the wide streets were impassable to traffic. Rubble was waiting to be taken away or even moved to one side. It seemed that the Berliners were losing the will to strive for a reasonable life. They were facing increasing numbers of bombing raids. The massive air raid on November 22nd had broken their hearts. And still the aeroplanes would come.

Much of Hufeland Strasse was untouched. At the further end Heinrich noticed several collapsed buildings. At this end, where his aunt lived, all seemed to be sound. They crossed the street and pushed open the double doors that gave entry to the central courtyard. Once in there, they looked up at the five floors. Hans asked where the lift was.

"There is no lift, Hans. We walk up the stairs. Let's count them," said Heinrich.

"I'm tired out," Hans sighed. For a seven-year-old child who had tramped across most of the city on foot, this was too much. Heinrich held open the door to let Maria through. Reluctantly, Hans followed. To him the climb lasted for ever. On the fifth floor, they met a pile of dumped furniture. Squeezing by, they came to number 9. The door was open a little. Heinrich looked puzzled.

"Giselle, Aunt Giselle," he called. No-one answered. He pushed the door open and went in. The flat was in turmoil. He realised very quickly that much of the furniture on the landing was hers. On the kitchen table was a pile of newspapers, and a box of china by the side. It was as though she had been packing. An old clock, several vases, and a collection of photographs in frames littered the floor. Of Aunt Giselle there was no hint or clue.

The family learnt from the people below that the old lady had begun packing her belongings two weeks previously. Then one day she simply disappeared. No-one could say what had happened. Heinrich realised that his message would never have reached her. Here they were, very weary from their experience of being bombed out of their own home, tired from a hazardous walk through the city and not even a welcome from a member of his family. Maria grasped the situation and straight away sorted through the kitchen to find something to drink and seek out anything to eat. She found enough to make some hot vegetable soup and served that to the three of them. The bread was dry and better dipped.

It took two weeks for Heinrich, Maria and Hans to settle there. They were unable to find any information about Giselle. They settled and waited. Heinrich, soon after their arrival, picked his way through many bombed streets to his place of work. There was little left of it. One or two of his colleagues were there attempting to recreate some order. Heinrich felt it would be a futile exercise. He told them where he had moved to, and returned to the flat.

The devastation of Berlin continued. Heinrich soon realised that to return to their ruined home, even to search through the rubble, was pointless. The streets were full of people who wandered aimlessly. The Schmidt's remained in the fifth floor flat, living on very little food. Water they had to fetch from a standpipe out in the street. When it was Hans's turn to fetch some, he could barely manage half a bucket up all of those stairs. Often much of it was spilt on the way back. Sometimes he would hide the empty bucket behind the huge doors onto the street. Then he would push one of the doors open to slip through. Over the next few months, he learnt to find his way through the streets. Nobody noticed him, for there were so many eight and nine-year-old children wandering, mostly made homeless.

He discovered that many families and old people were living amongst the rubble. Some had cellars for protection. Others used old doors to make shelters. So many seemed to have little will to go on struggling. On the street corners were loud speakers and Hans would listen to the Nazi messages telling everyone that victory

34

would be theirs. The Allies, the British, the Americans, the Russians, and all enemies of Germany would be beaten.

Often he heard the sirens wailing. If he was out, he would hide in the rubble and watch for the bombers coming. At first he was terrified. Now he had grown used to the explosions and the dust in the air. If the warning came and the family were in the flat, they often stayed there instead of running down to street level or sheltering in the cellars. They, too, had become numb to the dangers.

Chapter Six

The Russians Come

One day when he had wandered away from Hufeland Strasse, Hans came near to Alexander Platz at the centre of the city. He noticed smaller aeroplanes above, and very quickly realised that they were attacking each other. There had been rumours that the Russian army and airforce were getting close. He supposed that the fighters with red stars on their wings would be Russian.

The other sounds attracted his attention. These were not bombs, because he had seen no enemy bombers over the city that day. Yet there were explosions and, he thought, were coming from near the Brandenburg Gate. As he waited and watched, he began to be aware of more and more people passing by. Many were carrying suitcases or sacks tied with string. They all looked so old, so dirty, and so lost. More came and the streets were full of them, all going the same way. Hans caught a sense of their fear. He looked for someone to ask. He watched for a friendly face. The first person he approached pushed him away and shouted that he should run on. The next person mumbled, but he learned enough. The noise he was hearing was of Russian tanks shelling buildings. They were almost at Unter der Linden.

Suddenly he realised the danger that he was in. He ran back to the flat, cutting through the columns of refugees. There was chaos in Hufeland Strasse. German soldiers blocked the way. One, an officer, was shouting through a megaphone, demanding that everyone must stay and fight the Russians. A few men were nearby, clutching anything they could fight with. One carried a rifle. The others had heavy sticks, spades and a variety of metal objects. They were ill prepared to face the might of the Russian army. They looked thin, hungry, unshaven, and lost. Even the soldiers looked dejected. The officer who was berating everyone was the only person who seemed to have energy.

Hans wondered whether they would let him through the cordon to go home. He waited and watched for something to happen, to take their attention. He only had moments before a jeep came up the Greifswalder Strasse. The soldiers turned to stare at it, and at the cloud of dust swirling in its wake. It made them splutter and cough. Hans crept by through the cloud of choking dirt keeping along the edge against the wall. Once passed, he ran home to the flat. The large doors were open now, and he chased through the courtyard, into the inner hallway, up the stairs two by two. After three flights, he stopped, coughed, caught his breath and plunged onward and up.

The door to the flat was open. Heinrich was in the little kitchen, tying his bootlaces.

"Uncle, uncle," burst out Hans, "What is happening? Who are those people? Where do they come from? They are all so dirty and I can smell them."

"Hans, they are Berliners like us. They are running away from the guns. We think the Russians are coming." Heinrich glanced round to see Maria's expression as he added, "The Russians will set this city free."

"Uncle, there is nothing left to set free, and the guns are shooting at all the buildings and the army say you should fight the Russians and what will you use? You haven't got a gun."

Maria had been sitting at the table with a sewing basket of Aunt Giselle's. There was mending to do – a coat of Heinrich's, Hans's shirt, and so many socks. She realised that she had done nothing that afternoon. She sensed a change in the atmosphere. There had been a dull fear in everyone she had met. Some seemed to have lost any lustre for living; some began grumbling about conditions in the city. One or two mumbled against Nazi control of the country. Even to mumble was to incur the possibility of arrest for being a traitor to the Party. That meant prison, or work camp, or being shot. Maria looked back into Heinrich's face, trying to decipher his expression. Was he daft enough to join the other men at the street corner with their brooms and sticks?

"No, Hans, I will not fight – not even with a stick. It is too late for that. We are moving…"

Before Heinrich could finish, Hans burst in: "We cannot, Uncle. Can't you see? There is nowhere to go! Everything is bombed. This road is a lucky road because most houses still stand up."

"Come Maria, come Hans, bring all you can. We must go down into the cellars. Bring that water and all our food."

They understood, for this was no place to stay. Five stories above the ground gave them no chance should the building be bombed or shelled. They could have joined the column of refugees. Heinrich had decided that the dark, grimy cellar was better. They had enough to prevent starvation, nothing fancy. Rye bread, dry biscuits, and water had sustained them, and would continue to do so. The electricity had ceased to flow some days ago, and the water had to be fetched.

Hans clutched a bundle of candles, his bedding and a little bag of his treasures. He produced that from the back of a cupboard near his bed, but kept it away from the grown-ups. They noticed it, and wondered about its contents.

Between them they took down the essentials. In the cellar they joined various neighbours and others who, they suspected, had come in from the streets for shelter. It was crowded, and stifling. The air was stale and corners were lit with guttering candles. It was dry, and offered some safety.

That night no-one slept – or if they did, it was a fitful time. So in the early hours, when soldiers came crashing through into the courtyard, the cellar dwellers were alert immediately. They waited silently, fearful of what might happen. That silence was shattered with a burst of machine gun fire. It sounded very close indeed and seemed to be all around them. There was some shouting and a response. They heard the clomp of the soldiers' boots and then silence returned. No-one went out to investigate. They murmured quietly, speculating about the abrupt events.

Later that morning, when they yearned for coffee but settled for a tasteless imitation, Hans offered to fetch some water. It gave him cause to see this crumbling world for himself. He had become used to the sight of rubble and destruction.

The noise of aircraft continued to fascinate him, even with the chance of a bombing raid. That morning there were no wailing sirens. Hans looked up and saw some fighters circling overhead. In the distance was the rattle of gunfire. Nearer were the occasional heavy thumps of explosions and the collapse of buildings.

Then he heard chanting. The voices were young, perhaps children like himself. Maybe it was only in the next street. The soldiers had vanished and no-one was standing about waiting for the Russians. Hans clambered over the barricade, which he imagined had been constructed by those he saw yesterday. He wondered how grown-ups could build such a flimsy barricade and expect tanks to be halted by them.

Around the corner there was a group of children. They looked so ragged and poor. They were thin and stood in a straggly group. Hans ran toward them. As he did so, he could hear the chant: "Hitler kaput. Hitler kaput. Hitler kaput." They stopped whenever anyone came near. When that happened, they switched their chanting to plead for bread or anything to eat. They were ignored.

It was the end of April 1945 and the skies were clear – not entirely of aircraft, but certainly of cloud and rain. Hans felt some warmth from the shafts of sunlight that broke through the dusty layers. Maybe this sunny day brought the children out? He reached them and asked them what they were doing.

"Didn't you know? Hitler is dead. He's dead," they responded. Hans stared at them in disbelief. All through the war he had heard that name so often – daily on the wireless. As time went on, the name was spoken with increasing fear. The people of Berlin, and indeed of the whole country, had learned to fear their own leader. So many had disappeared through arrest or from curious midnight events. These had been those with the courage to speak against the country's leader, against the Nazi party and against the war. Here today, though, were children declaring the death of Hitler.

"It is true?" asked Hans, staring at these stragglers. He arrived back in the cellar having forgotten the water bucket. Later he found that it had been stolen. "Uncle, uncle, Hitler is dead," he declared.

All the conversations in the crowded cellar stopped immediately. After moments that seemed to last forever, someone asked him, "Did you say Hitler is dead?"

"Thank God," muttered an old lady, "Now there might be peace."

"What peace will there be?" burst out Heinrich. "He hasn't left us much to be peaceful about." Heinrich in that moment remembered his house in Stallupöner Allee. It was now rubble, as was most of Berlin. He glimpsed in his mind the model planes he had constructed and stored in the attics. They would now be bits of tin amongst piles of brick and mortar.

He had put the red plane in the cellar. And in that was his friend's plan. There was no hope of finding that. He sighed deeply and felt that he had let down Jakob and Anna, and so too, little Hans. In all the weeks and months of the war, there had been no word from there. Hans was no longer little Hans. He might be thin, but so were all the war people. Perhaps the Americans, the British, and the Russians were thin as well?

Hans had been with them for nearly seven years. Now he was nine. They had kept him safe through the ravages of bombing raids and the constant risk of his arrest. So far as Heinrich knew, no-one even suspected that Hans was a Jew. If Hitler is truly dead, he pondered, then perhaps the war, and this hideous destruction might soon end. Two days later the war did end. It ended, at least, for the Berliners. The city surrendered to the Russian forces. Most of the inhabitants felt an overwhelming sense of relief. The bombing ceased. They heard no more gunfire except for sporadic outbursts. They had little left. One and a half million Berliners were homeless. Food had almost run out. Russian troops were everywhere, but the evil of war had ended. That night in the cellar, Heinrich, Maria, and Hans slept soundly despite their hunger, thirst, and their longing to go home.

Chapter Seven

Blockade

The war was over. Berlin was a city of rubble. The Russians, under Marshal Zhukov, ruled the city and brought some order to the chaos. Trummerfrauen, the women of the ruins, worked at cleaning old bricks ready for reconstruction work. Food was rationed in very small portions, and the allowance per person was printed in the Russian press, Tagliche Rundschau. Workers would receive 600 grams of bread each day. Non-workers would have half of that. Most of the workers were women because the men had either been killed or taken prisoner at the Eastern Front. Little news of them found its way back into the city. And so the rubble was gradually removed to create new hills. One grew at Teufelsberg behind the ruined home that Hans had lived in for most of the war. It was called Rubble Hill.

Between those early weeks after the war and June in 1948, the Russians had increasing disagreements with the Allies: the British, French, and Americans. The city was divided into four sectors. The Russians controlled the Eastern part of the city, but regarded the whole city as under their government because it was deeply in their part of Germany. The Allies were not prepared to hand over West Berlin. These tensions came to a head when the Russians closed the borders. Their final act against the Americans was to halt a military freight train on its way into Berlin. Once halted, the Russian soldiers took up the rails in front of it. There was nothing that Major Lefevre of the U.S. Army could do.

So began the blockade of West Berlin. The roads and railways into and out of the city were blocked. It put West Berlin into a state of siege. The intention was to force the Allies to hand it over to Russian control.

The British response was to use an airfield at Buckeburg and others, then from these to fly in supplies to the two million people of West Berlin. It seemed a futile exercise when each Dakota aircraft could only carry three and a half tons. However, the Americans joined the struggle with their C54 Skymasters, each of which carried ten tons. Quickly, the operation increased until there was only a three-minute interval between each plane landing. The supply of aviation fuel became an . acute problem. So many flights demanded an incessant supply.

An exchange with the Russians was kept very secret. The deal was this: The Russians were very intent upon broadcasting propaganda through their radio transmitters; not only were these political programmes for the people in East Berlin, but aimed at the West Berliners, too. It was an attempt to demoralise them yet further, as if drastic shortage of food and the means of keeping warm were insufficient. However, the Russians found that their electricity supply was not enough for the broadcasting. In exchange for the flow of electricity from the Allies, they in turn were supplied with aviation fuel. One side could declare the benefits of Communism, whilst the other continued to overcome the siege of the city.

The West Berliners survived the siege, which ended on May 12th 1949, and celebrated the arrival of trucks by road and trains, too. There was a party mood and hope flooded back.

In amongst these desperate Berliners lived a few Allied workers, together with their families. We lived near the Olympic Stadium in a house on the sloping Reichsportfeld Strasse. Being only two years old at the end of the Blockade, I have no first-hand memory of those months. We lived, the four of us, for I had an older brother, in more comfort than the local people, but shared their deep anxiety. My father worked with the Control Commission for Germany and was engaged in restructuring the telecommunications networks – mostly telephones. It seems strange that we moved to Berlin so soon after the war to help the people whom we had regarded as our enemies. So it was with the Blockade. Pilots flying the food and coal into the city had been engaged on bombing raids over the same city not many months before.

One of those pilots, an American, became known by the West Berlin children as "Uncle Wiggly Wings". They looked eagerly for his aeroplane. As it approached Templehof, the airport in the centre of Berlin, the pilot would manoeuvre the aeroplane to give the impression of wiggling the wings. After that he would release sweets and chocolate through the bomb hatch. Hans lived in East Berlin. He missed this treat. So did I. I was too young and not a local Berliner.

Our home was requisitioned from the German owner. In other words, the British took it over for their own use. I suppose the army dealt with that. There we lived, and so came to know the city. Our house was warmed with a huge coal-fired boiler. This brute sounded like a cross channel ferry setting off! It needed feeding regularly and it made the house cosy in the icy winter.

Up the road from the house was the Olympic Stadium once favoured by Hitler for great rallies, political addresses, and stirring military displays. Since the war, its use as an athletics stadium had ceased. It had become the headquarters for the British Armed Forces. My dad worked there. Down the road was Heer Strasse, with a rebuilt tram system. The trams ran to the city centre, passing N.A.A.F.I., a shop for British military people. There were underground trains, too, like those in London. Over the road from Heer Strasse was Stallupöner Allee where Hans lived for a short time before the war, then during it until the house was bombed. Later we moved to that same road.

So the city was split. West Berlin, in which we lived, created a system of government similar to West Germany and the Allied countries. East Berlin, in which Hans lived, was becoming a Communist state. There was much talk of democracy and freedom, but the reality quickly became otherwise. Had Hans, with Heinrich and Maria, been able to stay in their own home, they too would have been caught up in the Blockade. Hufeland Strasse was in East Berlin. After the devastation of the war, the Schmidt family had to adjust to the rigours and fears of this new Communist state.

Heinrich returned to his work with the telephone system. Much of his time was now taken up in developing new networks for the enormous military presence. He travelled a lot and would come back late, bringing the day's tensions with him. Maria felt him change, but asked little. She suspected it was to do with the Russian influence.

Hans learned to keep quiet until Heinrich had had his supper. Hans had no space in the flat. He was twelve now, and growing. No Berlin children were fat, and Hans was thinner than most. His face had lost some of its wartime greyness, but with his short-cropped hair he still looked hungry.

He went to school and misbehaved. He and some other boys in the same class would slip out at lunchtime to roam the streets and watch the new building works around them. They found a corner shop where they stored cheap, ill-tasting cigarettes. One would be passed among them, mouth to mouth. At first it made Hans sick. The dizziness stayed long after he smoked. In time though, it became a habit which was kept away from home.

Occasionally he brought his friends home. They would crowd into the small living room and play cards or listen to the wireless. They found that sometimes they could listen to programmes broadcast from the West. Often, though, these were jammed. The Russians would send out a noisy signal on the same wavelength to prevent anyone in East Berlin from listening to it. But the boys tried and occasionally were successful. Their own programmes they found boring. The music was military and the talk seemed to be made up of endless political speeches. Both on the radio and in school, they were taught about the evils of capitalist Westerners. They learned quickly that it was better to agree and not to question, even though they suspected otherwise.

Even before the city had been divided, Heinrich found that it was impossible to go back to Stallupöner Allee in order to sift through the remains of their home. The streets were impassable and soldiers were everywhere. They were constantly checking documents and identity cards. Now he was living in the East part, he was prevented by police. It was becoming harder to travel anywhere, even from the East to the West of the city.

Having lost his collection of model aircraft in the bombing raid, he wanted to begin again. This time the models were a quarter of the size. The first he made entirely from scraps. This was old cans, wire and nuts and bolts. As he made it, he wondered if Hans would like to have it. Hans was beyond his childhood and would be leaving school. He knew Hans was eager to earn some money, partly for his own benefit but also to supplement the modest family income. He had, of course, outgrown his toys, though several he kept on his shelf.

As Heinrich pondered this, it occurred to him that he might insert a wrist watch mechanism into the model. This could act as the engine cowling and the hands as the propeller. It meant dismantling the fuselage and altering its shape. He did it using an old watch that a friend had repaired for him. This little model sat on its own undercarriage and the time could be read from the restored watch face. Remembering the Sopwith Camel he had modelled, he painted this one in the same coloured red paint. He was pleased with the result, even though this one did not contain the plan given to him by Hans's own father, Jakob.

The model was hidden, then, to await Hans's thirteenth birthday in the autumn. Even though East Berlin had not been subject to the Blockade, food was scarce and toys almost non-existent in the shops. Any manufacturing ability was given to continuing military products or goods for exporting.

Heinrich and Maria once enjoyed walking along Unter den Linden to gaze in the shop windows. Before the war, these had glittered with the finest goods from all around the world. Now the famous street looked barren. The rubble had gone, and much rebuilding had begun, and was continuing. Yet the shops looked so empty. Those that had displays looked forlorn. The shopkeepers could put their entire stock in the window, such was the shortage. This meant almost no choice of clothes, household wares, watches, or clocks. Times were hard, and made more difficult because the Russians had stripped the factories of essential machinery. This had been taken back to Russia, where the needs were urgent as well.

Hans had become as a son to Heinrich and Maria. He knew his own parents had been lost at the beginning of the war. He didn't know how this had happened or why. Neither had he asked. Sometimes he felt desperate to know and would spend anxious hours trying to find the courage to ask.

When he was younger, Maria talked to him and told him stories every night. She encouraged his music, although there was no piano in the flat. Hans continued to learn using an ill-tempered upright piano in his school hall. An old man living nearby offered to come in to the school out of hours and to teach any willing children. Hans was one of these, and although he enjoyed the company of the boys in his class, he would never miss a piano lesson or the opportunity to practise.

Hans's teacher, looking worn out and wearing a suit frayed at every edge, would come alive at the piano. Hans knew little about him, but loved the moments when his teacher would play. He watched the tired grey face sparkle. The piano, too, seemed to be in better tune for those moments. Sometimes Hans's friends mocked him. Once they littered the piano keys with old cigarette ends and the taped down the lid. On this occasion, the teacher, Herr Frentzen, tore off the strips of tape and lifted the lid, showing a degree of irritation. He was muttering as he did so. Then, as the lid sprang up, the stale ash ejected into a foul-smelling cloud enveloping the two of them. Amongst the splutters, Hans heard the sniggering laughter outside the hall window.

Hans's playing became too good for the poor school piano. One day, Herr Frentzen came to say that the lessons would continue using a grand piano in a small concert hall. As his skills increased, so did the friendship. His teacher took a fatherly attitude, which Hans found comforting. One day he spoke of his own adoption and the loss of his parents, of whom he had no memory. That caused the old man to stop the lesson and lapse into silence. His face fell and emanated a greater sorrow than his daily lost look. He took out a handkerchief, blew his nose and apologised. After another moment, in which the atmosphere was charged with emotion bordering on despair, he added, "You see, Hans, in that same year my wife was taken by the Nazis. All through the war I lived with the hope of her return. But as the months went by, my hope diminished. And now I know that she was taken to one of the camps. She died along with the others who were also Jews."

Hans was embarrassed and could not find a response. After failing to express his sorrow at this news, he suggested demonstrating his skill with a piece of Mozart. It was a lively piece, which lifted them both from reminiscing.

That night when Heinrich returned from work and the dishes remained by the sink, Hans found the courage to ask about his own mother and father. They were sitting at the kitchen table, which had space for only three people. The kitchen looked like a galley – very small, with a stone sink and rudimentary gas cooker. Most days there was a slight smell of gas, but getting someone to look at it seemed impossible. The table served for meal preparation, baking, for eating meals and for homework. The little kitchen was the heart of their fifth floor flat.

Heinrich answered Hans's nervous question. His reply was straightforward and without emotion. Maria sat still and watched Hans's face. He showed little response as the events leading up to Kristallnacht were related, followed by the disappearance of Jakob and Anna. The part of the story which Heinrich withheld was that of the plan lodged in the fuselage of the model aeroplane. Heinrich felt that if he spoke of the hidden stock of jewellery and watches, it would unsettle Hans. As far as Heinrich knew, the model Sopwith was crushed in the cellar and probably underwater from the rain finding its way through the rubble. To tell Hans might then tempt him to find their old house. That would mean travelling through West Berlin. Anyone moving through the city was still subject to on-the-spot searches, and merely crossing from East to West was all but impossible.

Hans listened to Heinrich. He didn't interrupt, but as the story of his own parents unfolded, he felt an immense sorrow descend on him. It seemed to envelop him in a fog of loss. He now knew what he had suspected. He was a Jew. Heinrich and Maria, he realised, had risked their own safety, even their own lives, by taking him in before the war.

When Heinrich finished, Hans lifted his head and said, "I'm going out." Maria reached over and tried to prevent him, but she was gently brushed aside. Maria saw from Heinrich's expression that they should let him out. They listened to him leave, and then Heinrich reached into the very back of the top shelf of the kitchen cupboard. He took out the red aeroplane in its box. "We'll not wait for his birthday," he explained to Maria, "I'll put it by his bed for when he comes in." They made a card, on which Maria drew a cartoon pilot holding the model. Inside they wrote a simple message: "Hans, we love you. Heinrich and Maria."

Hans clambered heavily down the flights of concrete stairs through the ill-lit stairwell. He shambled through the courtyard, in which the straggling conker tree was failing through poor light and very little penetrating rain. Later he realised that he had no idea of where he had wandered, except that he ended up at the foot of the huge brick built water tower at the end of Ryke Strasse. The tower was quite a landmark, standing taller than the nearby shops and cafes. Around it was a grassed park, very small now and rubble filled. The rain increased and pushed up dust from the mounds of one-time house fronts. Hans stood hard against the door into the base of the tower, sheltering from the downpour. After some moments staring out into the night, lit with the occasional streetlight, he sank to the threshold. There he remained only partially out of the wet. How long for, he did not know. He let the misery fill his heart.

Chapter Eight

Conscription1953

The water tower became a popular meeting point. It stood solidly at the edge of the small park, like a symbol of defiance. It had withstood the air raids of the war, when much of the surrounding area had been destroyed. Since then, two cafés had opened up over the road. These had soon become the favourite rendezvous of local young people. After work, they would greet friends, exchange news, talk politics in low voices or listen to the occasional busker. It was busy, with the tables on the pavements littered with glasses and cups. Ashtrays were spilling over with stubs, and the waiting staff were hard pressed to keep up with serving. And so these two cafés had become a password to anyone seeking company, but more so to anyone feeling ill at ease with the new Communist state that East Berlin had become.

Hans stepped out into Ryke Strasse to avoid the crowd of the first café. He crossed over to the park and looked for Lisa. Lisa had been at school with him, so they had known each other for several years. Lisa was the sort of girl who always had friends around her. Hans used to glance at her sometimes and wonder how anyone could be so friendly.

He and his own friends had always kept apart from the girls. As they all went up through the classes at school, they began to take more interest in them. Then one day last summer, in 1952, Martin had asked Elsbet to go to the cinema with him. It was the turning point for all of them. They each discovered that they could survive talking to the opposite sex.

Later that same week Lisa had an accident. She was knocked from her bike by a car. She broke her arm and for some weeks was weighed down by the thick plaster. The boys teased her endlessly about being defeated by a rusty old banger. "That wasn't a car," they said, "That was a wreck of a pedal car used for babies! How come it got you first?"

Hans found himself wondering about her, and decided that, at least, he could give her a "Get Well" card. He spent a long time finding one, and even longer deciding what to write. In a moment of courage, he wrote "Meet under the tower on Saturday afternoon?"

On Saturday morning, the group of friends again met at the café. Across the little tables which they had pushed together sat Lisa. She looked at him and thanked him for the card. Hans turned bright red, which brought a roar of laughter from the others. He glanced up at Lisa, and she mouthed, "Three o'clock." No-one else noticed or heard, such was the din.

At three o'clock, Lisa was not there. Hans was so disappointed. It would be their first meeting alone since they each left school. Whilst Hans worked hard, at least some of the time, he longed for the day when schooling would be past. Heinrich was very keen that he should go on to university. He should study Maths...

The elation and sense of freedom was lessened by this disappointment of Lisa's absence. They were going to meet and spend the evening at Maxim's. Hans stood by the tower door and looked about him. The last time he stood there, he remembered, was that awful night when he learned of his past. He remembered how he had sat hunched up for a very long time. Not long before dawn, he had crept home. Once in the flat, he dropped his wet clothes and crawled into bed. It was not until he woke up that he noticed the red aeroplane and the card by it.

Even though he, at his age, was not supposed to cry, he found the tears streaming down his face again. This time it was different. In the night, the tears were for the bitterness of loss, of never having known his own parents, at least not remembering them. This afternoon his tears were for the sense of relief that he had a family despite the tragedy. Heinrich and Maria had taken him in as their own son.

He looked up, realising that he had been staring at his feet. There, not two paces from him, stood Lisa. She smiled, "I've been here a few moments and you were far away in dreams." She took his hand and looked into his face.

"I'm sorry, Lisa," Hans blurted out, "I was missing you. I thought maybe you weren't coming."

"I had to go home for lunch. I set off early but it was the tram again. Always at Alexander Platz they stop and wait. No-one gets on. No-one gets off. The fat driver takes out his newspaper and reads. And no-one protests!"

Together they walked across back to the café. Hans glanced sideways at her. She always looked full of energy and ready for fun. Even cheap poor clothes looked good on her. Her auburn hair fell over her shoulders and her few freckles accentuated her small nose. Hans felt untidy next to her.

They found two seats and ordered coffee. At the next table were older people, engrossed in an argument over modern architecture. One was talking, somewhat too loudly, about plans to modernise the Platz where the trams screeched their way through the points.

Hans and Lisa talked quietly about the ending of their school days. Lisa could read in his face the feeling of liberation, of new hope, and somehow of new beginnings. She knew also that conscription would be imminent. He could not go straight to university or even to begin full time work somewhere. He would be required to join the army or maybe the police. They, the authorities, would decide which. It was compulsory for all young people. Conditions in the armed forces were harsh. In the police, it was a little better. Uniforms were issued, and endless orders followed. The pay was minimal and barely enough to send any home.

So all this clouded the recent freedom from his studies. It put a shadow over the lighter conversation. Hans led their talking to more distant hope, or maybe dreams. He described the model biplane by his bed. He told Lisa how his stepfather had made it from scraps, and how it had a clock in place of an engine.

"But it does more than tell the time," he continued. "It is my sign of freedom. It is a model of freedom, of flying in all the space above us. We were children in the war and that lasted for years. We were hungry and they fed us with lies. We wanted peace and they gave us terror. Afterward the Russians came, and now look." He swung his arm to show Lisa the other café customers. "We sit here and talk of politics because it is not safe to at work or at home. Soon it will be dangerous to criticise our government. Before the war, people disappeared, and in the war, too. Now it is whispered that the secret police will have more power."

"Hans. Hans, you worry too much. We are city people and we don't know the freedom that our country has. We should take the train to Petershagen and taste the air in the woods by the lakes. Then you will see that your plane is a sign of what we have now, even with the Russians here."

Hans sighed, "No Lisa. It isn't so easy. We think we are free but day by day it gets harder. Look at the papers and listen to what your neighbours say, or what you hear in this café. The two are not the same. The papers and wireless talk of a victorious new way for us in the East. But the whispering is different. My plane is a sign for times when the Russians have gone home, when we will live in peace and with a freedom that we have not known."

Lisa could detect a fire in Hans that was new. He had a far-sighted conviction of better conditions and hope. She wondered how he could survive the army or even the police force.

"If you could join the Vopos, our People's Police, you might stay here in Berlin to work. Then we could still meet. But the army..." She let the sentence lose itself amongst the chatter around them.

They walked back to the tram stop. There was drizzle in the air, which increased their anxious feelings for the future. They passed the ruined synagogue and Hans glanced at it. He wondered whether the few Jewish people would be allowed to repair it and use it for their worship once more. Somehow he doubted it.

Then with a sudden realisation, it occurred to him that he was Jewish, even though none of his official papers said as much. He knew very little of what it meant to be a Jew, except their terrible experience under the Nazis before and during the war. He wondered why it had happened and whether Jewish beliefs were so outrageous to other people. He almost commented to Lisa, but stopped. After all, she had no idea of this and he did not want to lose a special friend.

At the tram stop, they paused with an embarrassed silence. Neither spoke. Then the tell-tale metal screech preceded the train. Lisa looked into Hans's eyes. She touched his cheeks gently and climbed the steps. Hans waved as she was carried away into the night.

After that, they again met up and their friendship became full of trust as well as fun. Trust was a quality that became increasingly rare in this Communist state. The authorities were encouraging the public to report anyone they heard speaking against the government or any aspect of Communism. It was not long before individuals were arrested for subversion. Nevertheless, the cafés remained defiant.

In October, the postman brought a brown envelope bearing several official stamps on it. It was for Hans, and in it was a brief letter telling him to report to the army recruiting headquarters on the edge of the city. All summer, he had wondered about conscription. For him, and his friends, it was like waiting to go to the dentist. Each day brings a little more fear of what might happen. At the dentist, the agony lasts half an hour, he thought. With this call up to join the forces, it could stretch beyond three years. That would be three years away from his home, without his collections of friends, and he might well lose Lisa. The outlook seemed to cast a shadow even on the brighter aspects of his life. He did not relish the thought of wearing a uniform under Russian domination. He had three weeks until this appointment. He refolded the letter and leant it against his red aeroplane, blocking out the time. Then he moved it away and tossed it across the table. He would not have his sign of freedom hidden behind that foreboding letter.

When he told Lisa, he was downcast. On the day of the interview he was morose and very nervous. He deliberately wore everyday clothes and gave away very little about himself. He thought that if he sounded bright and full of ideas he might be posted far from Berlin, maybe even elsewhere in Eastern Europe. The interviewer tried to be relaxed and friendly. In Hans, he found a wall almost with no cracks. At last he collected up the various sheets of paper in front of him. As he pushed them into a file, he announced, "That will be all. You will hear within two weeks the result of this interview. Thank you for attending. Good day."

That was Hans's entry to uniform. He heard only five days later. He was to join the Vopos, the People's Police. He was given another three weeks before having to report to the barracks in Treptow at the southern end of the city. From then on, his life became full of having to report. There were daily reports, duty reports, reports on incidents, reports for the officers, copies for the Russians. When he was not on patrol, he seemed to have layers of faded brown and cream paper. Each sheet had the emblem of Communist Berlin at its head. He sat for hours in a drab hut under a bare light bulb, trying to think of anything to report. "I might as well report that I broke my bootlace today," he wrote to Lisa, "because no-one reads this stuff."

The days were long and the uniform itchy to wear. There were hours of standing near street corners along the boundary with West Berlin. At least checking the papers of passers-by helped to break the boredom. Barracks food was worse than he imagined possible. The cooks could do all sorts of recipes using cabbage. The taste was always the same – a bland, lukewarm boiled texture. The smell wafted through everywhere so that even his uniform stank of cabbage. It was little wonder, he thought, that he smoked far more. At least the tobacco had some stronger flavour.

He disliked his new life. It was regulated with orders from aggressive and dissatisfied officers. Never was his uniform smart enough or his reports full enough. Thank you was a response that became obsolete. He had to make a hard effort on his visits home to express thanks. Grumbling became normal between the men. They mistrusted the officers and trusted one another even less. Hans wondered how many of them wrote reports against other members of the Vopos.

As Christmas approached, the days shortened and often the temperature was below freezing. He wore his own clothes under the uniform in an attempt to keep warm. Amongst his fellow policemen there was superficial friendship. Jokes and cigarettes were shared. Drink of any alcoholic description was strictly forbidden. Hans noticed that many of them kept a small bottle of spirits hidden in a pocket. They would suck peppermints to disperse the smell on their breath. At least the drink was warming, even if only for a few moments.

The Communist state tried to dismiss Christmas and carry on forcing the lazy machinery of East German industry to churn out poor quality goods for ill-stocked shops. Despite this, Hans found he could have some days at home over the festival. He heard this in early December and began counting off the days until Christmas Eve.

Nearer to Christmas an officer came into the canteen as Hans and his patrol were eating, or chewing, their cabbage-based stewed meat. Captain Heinemann was carrying a large cardboard box which was tied with string.

"My good men," he announced. Hans nearly choked. He had never heard of such praise, and immediately became suspicious.

"You must have girlfriends, you have mothers and grandmothers. And it is the season for giving presents." No mention of Christmas, Hans noted. The string was untied and the officer drew from the box a woollen scarf with a checked pattern. There were others, and the variety was spread over two tables.

"I have this consignment," the captain said. "They come from Scotland and I offer them first to you." Hans wondered how they had come from Scotland. Someone must have brought them across from West Berlin. And before that, who could buy a large box full of woollen scarves? The quality was far better than that of any in the East Berlin shops. One of Hans's patrol began to ask about them and was stopped halfway through his question.

"It is foolish to ask," said the captain, "You like these? Then you can have one for only twenty-one Marks." Hans gasped. It was nearly two weeks' worth of spare money, two weeks' worth of cigarettes, drinks, cinema tickets and tram fares.

"You have a girlfriend?" Hans reddened, as though the captain had seen his very thoughts. Then someone called over that he would buy one. Another was picked up and paid for. Very quickly the pile was diminishing. Hans acted before it was too late. He chose a red checked scarf for Lisa, drew out his wages and paid.

So Christmas came. Hans hid his uniform under his bed so that he would not be reminded of the end of this festive holiday. He had wrapped the scarf carefully and put it under the small Christmas tree. His presents for Heinrich and Maria were less expensive, but he had chosen them carefully: a new modelling saw for Heinrich and a set of biscuit cutters for Maria. He hoped she might try them whilst he was there.

He took his gift for Lisa with him on Christmas Eve. It was late in the evening when he nervously rang the bell at the foot of the block of flats where she lived. Her father spoke through the intercom and released the door. Hans ran up three flights of stairs and, with his head down, almost knocked Lisa over. She had come out to stand by the stairs to greet him.

He felt the warmth of her embrace, and realised how much he missed her company, her fun, and seriousness.

They spent two very special hours walking through the city streets, hand in hand and with a lightness in their hearts. Hans knew then that he never wanted to lose her but could not find the words to say as much. He hoped she felt the same. Christmas in 1953 gave Hans a colourful holiday amidst the drab, cold, dark times of duties and report writing in the People's Police. He was now seventeen, and as a Jew, had survived the terrors of Kristallnacht, the war years and post-war Communist state of East Germany. In his heart, he knew there was freedom to be found, preferably with Lisa.

Chapter Nine

Coffee and Biscuits 1955

It was snowing. The icy wind whipped up the flurries of snow into whirlwinds at the street corners. Coming home from work, Hans had his coat buttoned high and he sunk his chin into it to keep a little warmth. He almost closed his eyes so he could still see enough without feeling the stinging cold. His face ached with the sub-zero temperatures. He passed others on the way but noticed no faces or familiar greetings. His only thought was to reach the courtyard of the flat and climb the stairs to the warmth of the kitchen.

Maria made coffee but before the aroma reached Hans, he could smell biscuits cooking – ginger and spice, he hoped. As a child, he used to watch Maria press them out of a wooden mould. They would be flat, in the shapes of windmills, pine trees and decorated wooden houses.

"How was it today, Hans?"

"Not good, Maria." Hans, when he was younger, called Maria 'Aunty.' Now she had persuaded him to use her Christian name. At first he was saddened because it meant leaving behind some of his childhood. The biscuits, at least, continued.

"No, my patrol was sent to the flats in Mentzel Strasse. We had to arrest a woman, and she had three little children in there. We're not told what the crime is, but the office said it was to do with subversive literature. There was nothing there. We found no capitalist magazines, nothing American, and no English papers. The children were so frightened. They cried and ran into the bedroom. When Bernardt went in there to search, they screamed. Oh Maria, this cannot be right. If I question it at the barracks, I get into trouble at the barracks and they threaten to tear off my corporal's stripes."

Maria said quietly, "Hans, it is not right. It is not our way in the family. It is not right for us as German people, as Berliners. We have had those terrible years under Hitler, and the Jewish people were taken away. We have had war, and lost our homes. Now with the promise of a new freedom and a new equality, we have fear spreading. Ordinary people are frightened. Even in their own homes, they dare not speak of anything criticising the state. Children in our schools are asked what their parents talk about at home. Then come arrests. Oh Hans! Must you do it?"

She looked at him with anguish on her face. As he worked out his reply, she drew the tray of biscuits from the oven. Hans found himself caught up in the two worlds; the remnant of his childhood with the warm spicy smells, and the cruelty of the new Marxist state.

"I was called up and made to join the People's Police."

"But you are still in it!" Maria was angry now. "You could have left. You are one of them."

"Yes, I am." Hans sighed deeply and leant forward to rest his arms on the table. "I am in it and each day it gets worse. At first it was cold work and poor pay. There was so much corruption and black marketing. Now I and a corporal, and we are sent to families to take away a father or a mother. We see the faces of the children as we do it. We see their tears and their fear. And the authorities tell us that we do such important work for our government."

"But you can get out." Maria looked at him and her eyes were pleading.

"Yes, I could. Today we took away the mother. I suppose the father was at work somewhere. The old couple on the floor below collected those scared little children. They said they would keep them until their father came home. I have broken a family, Maria."

They fell into a silence of sadness. Maria poured the coffee and they tried the biscuits, warm and spicy.

"Soon I can ask for a transfer to different work. In June we have a review and we can request a move. If I say it is for me to gain new experience in the police, I think it will help. But others will go on arresting and spreading fear. All for the glory of the Marxist state."

"You must change, Hans, because then you will sleep better. Your conscience will be quieter. What would you do?"

"Office work, paperwork arranging arrests. No, not that. I will ask for border work. It will be checking anyone wanting to go into West Berlin, or anyone coming this way. That will mean some patrol work, and some office work. Maybe the office work will be in the winter. I could feed old forms and scrap wood onto the fire and keep warm!"

The conversation ended. As they enjoyed the biscuits and coffee, they each wondered how different it might be in the West.

Chapter Ten

Plans for a Tunnel 1955

In the West, it was different. Berlin showed how great the division was. In America and Western European countries there was a struggle, but families had a better time. As each year went by, jobs were more plentiful and new ideas flooded the shops. There was colour and hope and holidays. In the East, or the Communist Block behind "the Iron Curtain", life was increasingly drab and driven by fear and uncertainty. From East Berlin, it was possible for Hans and others to catch glimpses of better living in the West.

In West Berlin, stories were abundant about the poverty, the arrests and the work of the People's Police. Suspicion increased between the two sides. So began the years of the Cold War, with Russia and America stalking round each other like two fighters ready to pounce.

Because my dad worked for the British government in Germany, we lived in West Berlin. He never talked about the work, so I had to guess. In the morning he would go to the office, and come home usually about six o'clock. Sometimes he would go away for a few days. Then he would send us a postcard, but wrote very little on it. He was not away for a holiday, but I could not understand what type of work he would do in Damascus or Beirut, Libya, or London.

We had now moved to a different house in Stalluponer Allee. One day, the house was tidied up and everything had to be put away. My toys were behind the cupboard doors. All I could do was wander from room to room and wonder. Then mum explained. "Tonight," she said. "People are coming from the office. They are having drinks. If you like, you can help now. "

So I carried and fetched and, I suppose, I was helpful. Really it was a way of stopping me saying, "Mum, I'm bored. What can I do?"

Usually when I complained like that, she would say, "You've got a great big garden – go and play in it." Or, "Go and play in your room." But today was different. There was a bustle. Mum and the maid, Anna, washed and cleaned everything everywhere. Boxes arrived full of bottles and glasses. The front garden was trimmed, the grass cut and a sign put up: *Stallupöner Arms.* I wondered why the street needed arms. No-one explained that it was supposed to resemble a pub that you might find in England. So Stallupöner Allee, the road, now had a temporary pub!

Next door on one side lived an old German couple. I hardly ever saw them. On Sundays, they would dress up very smartly. They would go out in the morning and then again about three o'clock. I learnt that in the morning they went to church, but not to ours. In the afternoon they would visit their favourite café for coffee and cakes. On this day, Anna was sent to explain to them that we were having a party and so there would be more cars parked along the road.

We had no neighbours on the other side. That house had been bombed in the war, so my dad told me. Through the hedge, I could see where the downstairs floor had been, and the piles of rubble grown over with bramble and fireweed. Sometimes I wished I was brave enough to push through the hedge and explore. Maybe, like our house, it had a cellar.

That night, everyone came. The house was crammed and the noise increased until it was hard to hear anyone say anything. But I did hear my dad tell me to take Mr Blake's briefcase from him and put it in the study. I did, and while I was in there I noticed a whole pile of cigarettes. Each packet was wrapped in clear cellophane. My dad smoked cigars. But these! If these were handed round, the place would stink for the next year.

Carefully, so carefully, I separated the cellophane, took the cardboard box and tipped out the cigarettes. I wanted to hide them – but where? Every drawer was locked. Then I noticed the briefcase. Was it open? Yes, and so I tipped the contents of the first three packets in there. As I did so, I noticed typed sheets of paper and part of a map. On the map, I noticed because I was nosy, was Schönefelder Chaussee and nearby other streets I had never heard of, and an American radar base. I remembered that my day had his car mended in a garage along one of them. The garage man had given me a little Mercedes badge to wear on my pullover. I wondered what car Mr Blake had come in.

Then my attention went to the typed pages. They looked boring, except that at the top in red was stamped 'Secret' and under that 'Operation Gold'. Was he a doctor who did operations? No, because that one word seemed to spring from three places on the pages. That was the word 'tunnel'. A door opened and I heard conversation nearby, and footsteps. I pushed the papers back in, closed the briefcase, but had no time to tidy up the cigarette packets. I wanted to slide the cellophane wrappers back over each so they looked new again.

Instead, I slipped out of the study, feeling very guilty and scared. I was sweating and I shook a little. What if Mr Blake had seen me? I ran upstairs and shut myself in my bedroom.

Later, I crept back down. From the stairs, I could see Dad talking to Mr Blake. He seemed to be called George. I guessed that they hadn't seen the cigarettes. Holding my breath till I was bursting, I went back to the study. By now my hands were so shaky that it took quite a few minutes to make the packets look real again. What a great relief I felt that no-one had been into see them. I did nothing about those cigarettes that I had dropped into the briefcase. There wasn't time. I slipped back out into the kitchen hoping for something to eat.

The following day, Mum and Anna spent clearing up. It was one of those horrible days where you are always in the way, so I stayed in my room most of the time. It was better at suppertime. Dad came home and the family sat around the table eating, and talking a little. Thank goodness nothing was said about the missing cigarettes! Later, when I was on the landing, I could hear Mum and Dad talking. I heard Dad say "Operation Gold". I stood absolutely still and listened carefully. I think Dad was telling Mum about his work and that he had to go to a big place near Schönefelder Allee – something about radar and the American Army...

I knew Dad went to the office. We sometimes met him there. Nearby was the Olympic swimming pool, where we could swim. I stayed at the shallow end and often watched others diving off the ten-metre board. I couldn't understand how anyone could find the courage to do it. Afterward we would climb up onto the statues of lions whilst we waited for Dad to meet us.

I had a feeling that this radar place he talked about was near to the garage. I wondered what radar looked like and whether I could go with him. And was the radar to do with the tunnel that I read about on the typed papers? I very quietly crept back to my room. Maybe tomorrow I could tell my friend Chris.

Later, I discovered this was part of the Cold War.

The 'Cold War' between America, Britain, and other NATO countries, and the Communist countries was one without fighting. The armed forces were 'on alert' and ready for action both night and day. There was a constant risk of nuclear war, so it was important to know what the enemy was planning. Both sides used spies to gather vital information. The Russians and East Germans would spy on the Western countries, especially America and Britain. In return, they would try to collect military and political information from the Communists.

One way that worked well was Operation Gold. The C.I.A., which was the American spy network, worked with M.I.6, the British equivalent. They planned to dig a long tunnel from West Berlin into East Berlin and then connect up to the telephone cables in the East. These carried a vast number of military messages and conversations. It was a dangerous mission because if it were found out, it could provoke 'a military response' – in other words, war.

Dad's job was to find out where the military cables ran, and to prepare plans for the tunnel. He already knew Herr Schimmel, an important Post Office engineer in Berlin. Herr Schimmel had old plans from before the time of the Communists. These helped considerably, but there were gaps. Captain Wallace, a US soldier, sent extra plans of Berlin from his base in Heidelberg. Where they were found, no-one seemed to know. It was clear that if the tunnel could reach under the Schönefelder Chaussee, in the district of Rudow, then with care the tunnellers could dig up and fix listening devices to the cables without damaging the telephone system. In that way, the telephone conversations could be recorded and sent for translation from Russian and German into English.

The problem was how to dig a tunnel of about five hundred metres without being noticed. There were constant Russian and East German patrols using that road. They would notice any lorries coming, and going laden with waste soil. The answer was to use an American warehouse which housed radar equipment. It was close enough and large enough to hide all the tunnelled rubble. The tunnel would pass near to a cemetery, under a ploughed field and the barbed wire boundary.

American tunnellers dug it five metres down, going out from the warehouse basement. They had practised at Longmoor military base in England because there the soil was very sandy, too. As the tunnel progressed, it was lined with steel sheeting and sandbags. The sandbags offered some insulation. Any water would be pumped out.

Where the tunnel passed under the boundary between East and West, steel doors were fitted to a special room full of amplifiers, set on special shelves. The banks of tape recorders which were linked to these produced eight hundred reels each day. They were sent to a base at Regents Park in London and to Washington Mall in Washington in America. Other steel doors sealed this section. Within the recording room were lengths of garden hose filled with plastic explosives. They would be detonated if the enemy ever found their way in. On the steel door at the boundary was a notice in both German and Russian stating 'Entry is forbidden by order of the Commanding General.'

The final part was the connection to the telephone lines that ran beneath the road surface. This meant digging upward, hoping the ground would not collapse into the tunnel. It meant, also, knowing exactly where to dig up. After all, only a one metre mistake would be too much.

The whole project, 'Operation Gold', was ready to begin listening and recording Russian and East German military phone calls in April 1955. It had cost thirty million dollars, and its success was vital.

I suppose we had, as a family, difficult times when Dad would come home very tense and nervous. But I didn't understand why, and obviously, he could not say. Spies do not talk about their work. Maybe he only told Mum where he went on some occasions. The day did come when he could relax. The tunnellers had found the cables, connected up and were ready to record. Dad, Mr Blake, and the others had been successful so far. On April 10th, the tape recorders began their work, and all went well for eleven months and eleven days. Then, the East Germans and Russians discovered it.

Chapter Eleven

The Cellar Next Door

I wondered why we, that is the British, had to bomb the house next door in the war. Was it a secret base? Was it where Hitler lived? It was later that I realised it must have been a stray bomb. When you watch films about the war, the bombs always seem to hit the target. Really, they were not very accurate and very many landed and exploded elsewhere. Some didn't explode, and some may even be lying hidden today.

The only remaining part of that house was the downstairs floor and, I supposed, the cellar. From what I had been able to see through our hedge, there was nothing but rubble. Out of the rubble had grown so many brambles that there seemed to be a miniature hill. This hill, in the summer time, was covered with fireweed as well as the impenetrable prickly bramble. The proper name for fireweed is Rosebay Willowherb. There is also a long Latin name for it. But its nickname fitted well. It would grow so easily wherever there were ruins. The tall straggling plants with pink flowers would cover burnt out house ruins and bombsites. They would give the impression of flames when they flowered in the summer.

In the next road lived Chris. He was a good friend at home and in school. We seemed to understand each other. We could 'muck about' one minute and switch to serious talk the next. Sometimes he would come with us for family outings. His dad was a teacher at the school, but he was alright. I was waiting for him one day. I suppose I was bored indoors, and outside it was sunny. Berlin could get so very hot and stuffy in the summer, and then we would have the most enormous thunderstorms. In the winter, it could get so cold that it would hurt your face and make your hands ache. The snow would come and would stay, covering everything with a thick white blanket. But today was good. It was warm and a bit windy.

Chris came and said polite things to Mum, and then we went out. I told him about the ruin next door, so we both peered through the hedge to see.

"What do you think? Shall we do it?" I urged him on so that I could be brave in his shadow.

"Come on, let's." His answer caught me out a bit because somehow it seemed wrong, and could be dangerous. By the time we had broken through the hedge and climbed the wire fence, we were badly scratched. We found sticks to bash the brambles out the way. I was looking for the cellar steps because there was nothing else left. Though I did wonder if under all the wiry mess of bramble, there might be finding something to find amongst the rubble.

Chris called me over. He had pushed through and had found a gap in the floor. Some blocks were too big to move but we managed to make the hole big enough to squeeze through. That was the easy bit.

"What do we do now?" I asked, knowing the answer.

"Go into it," he said. "You first."

The hole was uneven and black. We poked sticks down and felt what might be steps.

"Get a torch." That meant the horrible scramble back through the hedge, an excuse to borrow our big torch on a sunny day, and the return push over the fence. Chris stayed behind. It took me quite a long time, and he had started to come back to look for me.

"You were ages."

"My mum saw me with the torch. I told her we had made a den down at the bottom of the garden. Come on, let's go back."

Torchlight showed us nothing. The sunlight was too strong. The only thing to do was to squeeze through the gap and try to climb down. That was the trouble. It was easy to be brave before. We could encourage each other and say strong things, but now with this black hole at our feet, it was different. I was beginning to feel a bit scared. I wanted to suggest that we go back and do something else when Chris said, "I'll squeeze into this bit, feet first. Then my head will still be up here."

Wasn't he scared? Didn't he feel a bit sick, as I did? I felt prickly with it all. Anyway he did it. I held the torch and he wriggled down to waist height. "Then what?" I thought. He will have to go right down in to the blackness.

"I've got the torch. Say when you need it."

Chris said, "Make sure you stay here. Don't go away, don't move."

His head disappeared. Then a muffled voice called for the torch. I reached down the hole with it and he took it.

"The smell down here is disgusting, but otherwise it seems alright. Are you going to come, Hugh?" If he, my friend was already down there, how could I not go?

With the help of the yellowing torchlight we found that the steps were manageable. Some rubble was in the way but at least we could see it. There was such a mess down there, and water, too. Our feet got wet, so I supposed the rainwater had collected in puddles. We noticed that, apart from the water, mud and dirt, everything was there. In other words, there were doors and light switches. We tried to open one door. It wouldn't move. Maybe it was locked, or even damaged from the bomb. And the years of dampness may have made the door stick fast. The worst thing down there was the sweet and sickly smell. It seemed to get worse, the longer we were down there.

"Let's try the other doors." Chris's voice sounded dull. I think he was feeling frightened after all! I was, too. But we found the next one opened. Inside, the torchlight showed wooden boxes and lots of tools. All of them were rusted and most were gardening implements. The boxes had lids which came off easily. We were disappointed. They were storage boxes for nails, nuts and bolts, screws, and scraps of metal and wood.

"Not much here," I commented. "Try that door behind you." It was stuck, but Chris fetched a spade and pushed it underneath. Suddenly it swung toward us and he fell back against the wall. The torch fell but was not damaged. I picked it up and shone it on him. He was filthy. He was black and covered in cobwebs. His face was streaked with a sooty mess.

"You look a complete mess," I said and laughed. He struggled off the floor and together we peered into this room. It was full of more boxes around the walls. But there was also some furniture set out. It was as though it had been a sitting room. A small table in the middle had chairs around it. Up on a shelf we found cups and plates. Then behind the chairs were boxes of tinned food. The labels were mildewed and came off as we touched them. There was rust at the edges. We found the remains of packets of dried peas, of flours and biscuits. They must have been eaten by mice, or even rats. I pulled away another chair. I was feeling braver now, even in this down underground place. I shone the torch at other boxes. Then what caught my eye was a little propeller. Could it be a toy aeroplane? A cloth covered the shape. I pulled it off to reveal a lovely model biplane. It was painted red and covered in filthy cobwebs.

"Chris, Chris, look!" I showed it to him.

"Cor, that's lovely. That's a real treasure. You ought to keep that."

"It's not mine. It might belong to someone," I said.

"But it's been here for years. Everything has. If someone wanted it, they would have come to fetch it. Maybe the people who lived here were killed in the war."

What Chris said excited me. I could keep it. I took it down and put it on the table. Together we searched for other treasures. We found none except some little children's toys. I could tell that Chris was disappointed. I found the plane and he wanted something, too. I suggested he took some bits of china – a cup, saucer and plate. He did. Much later he discovered their worth. The mark under each was Dresden, a very famous German china factory.

Somewhere, a long way from us, a voice called. It was my mum. We collected up our bits, and using the last of the fading torchlight, made our way back to the steps. The sunshine was so dazzling after our subterranean exploration.

Mum was horrified and she was angry, too. We had hidden our treasures at the back of the garage, but we couldn't hide our filthy and scratched selves!

The red plane became one of my favourite toys. I never played with it, but kept it at the front of the shelf in my cupboard. I learned that it was a Sopwith Camel, but painted with the wrong colour. It was my treasure.

Chapter Twelve

Finding the Warehouse

I was scared. I was scared because Nick had told me about what had happened to someone he knew. They went to the dentist, the same one that I had to go to, but the drill had missed the tooth, making a hole in the top of his mouth instead. Nick was three years older than me and always knew what to say to make me frightened. I hated him.

I was scared too because it hurt. You climb into the chair, and already you are sick inside and shaking outside. My mum would tell me a few days before a visit to the dentist. From that moment, each day would be ruined by my terror. And on the morning of the appointment, I would keep my head under the bedclothes, pretending to be sound asleep. If I could stay there for long enough, maybe Mum would forget. It never worked!

So my life was broken with visits to him, his poking tools and the ghastly grinding drill. Inevitably the day came around again. I would climb up into the chair. With my head held back and my mouth open, I already wanted to swallow. The system of belts and pulleys was still. So, no drilling, not yet. The dentist poked each tooth from one side of my mouth to the other, one hurt, and I flinched. I tried to disguise it so the dentist would move on to the next one. Oh no, he saw it. My fear was worse. Already I could visualise the belts moving and the drill making its hideous grinding noise.

"Open wide," he said, "And if it hurts, lift your arm."

My stomach knotted up. I clenched my fists and screwed my eyes shut. And it hurt. The pain seemed to go all around my head. I lifted my arm. The pain was worse. And the drilling went on. Had he seen my desperate plea to stop? "One more little bit," he said.

The best part of being in the dentist's chair is when he pushes the soft filling into the tooth. It must be like pushing wet sand into a seaside bucket.

"Have a rinse now." Then I am released from this abject misery for another six months.

Afterward, I was allowed to choose a comic to bring home. There was a paper shop nearby that was part of NAAFI, shops for the forces people. I would look along the bottom rack at the brightly coloured offerings: Beano, Dandy, The Eagle, Girl and Swift. These were happy moments of release, which were only ruined if the dentist said I had to return for more work.

When we got home, Anna had made soup for lunch. She was so good at that. I always looked forward to her days with us. Today she had put out German bread. It looked grey and tasted so different. But I liked it, especially with butter from the fridge spread thickly on it.

As we were eating, Mum asked Anna to look after me the next afternoon. She had some official social engagement and would not be back before six o'clock. I suppose that meant afternoon tea and then cocktails for her. Anna's face fell and she explained that she had planned to visit her sister. It would be her day off. It would be nearly the anniversary of her own mother dying and together the sisters would visit the cemetery. Mum looked irritated by that, but then Anna brightened.

"Hugh comes with me. Nearby there is a park on a hill. There we will have some ice cream." She could speak good English, I thought.

Mum asked where this was. Anna explained that it was in a district called Rudow. So it was settled.

The ride on the underground train was very long but I enjoyed the journey. After a while the train ran overground so I could watch out of the window. Anna had with her a street map and during the journey I asked her to show me where we were going. I looked over her shoulder. Every time the train bumped, her pointing finger would slide a mile or two on the map. Anyway, we found the street and as I looked another name sprung up at me: Schönefelder Chaussee. As I looked, also saw marked Schonbergweg. Why, I wondered, did I notice that and not others?

Inside I felt a touch of excitement but could not understand why. Anna put away the map when she noticed that I was staring into the distance. Had we learnt something at school? Had Dad talked about it? Then with a flash of memory I had it. That very street name was on the papers in Mr Blake's briefcase.

Immediately the afternoon out changed from a pleasant ride, with the promise of boredom in a cemetery and then ice creams, into something more. Now I wanted to explore.

From the underground station we walked to Schrimmerweg. On the way, I said to Anna that my dad had his car mended somewhere nearby and the garage man was friendly.

"We'll look for it," she said. "We'll make it fun. I know some streets here but no garage. We'll go hunting for it." My hopes rose because I might see the American radar base that was on Mr Blake's map. Could the tunnel be there?

Together with Anna's sister, we went to the cemetery. They brought flowers at the corner shop and put them down where their mother was buried. She died, they explained, right at the end of the war when the Russians came through the city. Anna and Heidi were twelve and fourteen then, and were caught up in the street fighting. Their mother thought it was safe and so they followed her over the road back to their flat. A stray bullet hit her as she reached the front door. Anna and Heidi screamed. In that instant, the two of them were made orphans.

They cried at the graveside, and I was embarrassed. I wandered off, trying to invent a game to pass the time.

Armed with ice creams, we then went in search of the garage. I insisted on holding the map, and pretended I knew more or less where to find it. I didn't, but I led the three of us right past the American radar base.

I noticed that the main gates were shut and one American soldier was guarding it. He had a sentry box but was walking backward and forward before the gates. I supposed that if it were to rain hard, he would stay in it and watch from there. I wished I could go in and look. Anna and Heidi looked at the guard. He smiled at them. Anna went red and Heidi giggled. Maybe they could ask him.

They didn't. Instead, I let my imagination wander. We went back to Heidi's house for tea and then set off home. It was a lucky day.

Chris and I met at school after our half term holiday. I told him of my trip. We agreed we should try to find a way in to discover the tunnel. That became our secret. Our planning and dreaming occupied most of our spare time together.

For the next two weeks nothing happened. I suppose we were busy at school. And at home we had spent the evenings in. Even though it was lighter for longer, it was still so cold. There were some harsh frosts and on the hills behind my house there were pockets of snow clinging to the earth, waiting for the springtime warmth. This winter there had been a lot of skiing on a specially created slope. I could watch them from my bedroom window, but before long my attention would wander. After all, each skier did the same route. There were no jumps or tricky turns, just a long straight run.

Now, sledging was more fun. More fun because we did it, and we made our own run in the woods. We called all that area 'the woods', but it was not all wooded. There were areas that were very open and hilly. It was here that we made our own run. We found some old tyres which we piled up and packed with snow and formed a slope. To jump two was possible. We never managed three. We would end up in the deeper snow, bruised and shaken. At first our run would be slow. Greasing the runners helped. What was better, though, was treading the snow down to an icy track. Each day, with wear, it would get faster. My sledge was a small size and after a few runs and two tyre jumps, it lost some of its strength. I suppose the joints were loose. It didn't stop me. I kept that sledge for a very long time – years in fact.

In the spring, our sledges were tucked away in the loft. But we had scooters with pump up tyres. These went well over the sandy paths that criss-crossed the woods. In our imagination they could be motorbikes with radios, and we would search out the enemy.

As this springtime was still so cold, the bedroom carpet formed the battleground for toy soldiers and tanks. Sometimes the patterns on the carpet made roads for cars and lorries. Now, as the days went by, the visit with Anna seemed so absurd. There really couldn't be a way into the tunnel. It would be heavily guarded; there would be soldiers all over the place. No, we couldn't do it. We would be too scared even to go through the gate if it was open. I was thinking this and wondering why people called it 'having cold feet' when the doorbell rang. It was Chris. Other than at school, I had not seen him much since my trip with Anna. I guessed that he too found the idea ridiculous.

He knew where to find me, and I heard him call from the stairs. He ran into my room and dived onto the bed. "Guess what, guess what?" he burst out, "Dad's got car problems. You know our stupid car. It's a make no-one has heard of and the garage is miles away. He has to take it there and said I could go. I didn't want to. It means hanging around for ages while they fix it. But I remembered something. You know you went with your maid, Anna, that day and you passed that old water tower with the huge DDR on it? I think it is near the garage. If it is, it will be near the tunnel, too."

It took a moment for me to realise what he was saying.

"Don't you see? If you could come, we could clear off while my dad waits. He likes their special room with its old magazines to look at. What do you think?"

What did I think? I was scared. It is alright to dream of what you might do – that is all safe stuff. But to have a day when you can! "We can't. We haven't got anything ready, Chris."

"Yeah, there's time. All we need is a torch and some old clothes. Go on, say you'll come."

I was cornered. It was my idea in the first place. But when I thought it up, I was in bed, warm and dreaming of all sorts of schemes. What should I say? Maybe on the chosen day I'd be going out somewhere else. For a briefest moment even going to the dentist would have been an excuse. "I s'pose," I said, probably sounding very reluctant. "When's he going?"

Chris's dad wanted to get the car in that lunchtime. Soon we were on the way. His car was so bumpy. I think they called it 'Goliath'. Maybe it was a joke because it was so small. But in the city it was alright. The journey was stop, start, stop, start nearly all the way. It was one of those days when the traffic lights were always red. In one or two places there were still old fashioned box lights. We passed one. It is a box in the middle of the crossroads, hanging from the wires. Each of its four sides had one hand, like a clock in a way. As it turned, it would point to either a red or a green area. So you watched it, like the clock, and set off as the hand moved from the red to the green quarter. I guessed that the trouble with the car was to do with the gear box. There was a metal scraping noise whenever his dad changed gear.

At the garage there was chaos. Someone was shouting at the mechanic and cars blocked the road. We stopped by the showroom. "Dad, what time shall we be back?"

It wasn't far at all to the high fence and the gate protecting the yard by the warehouse. We could see the radar dishes and numerous aerials on the roof. In the yard were crates in great piles and a few military vehicles. There was a soldier gazing over the road beyond the rough ground. Far away were blocks of flats, modern at that time. From the warehouse they looked like wooden bricks from a toy box. I wondered what it would be like to live there. We were told all sorts of stories about what it was like to live in East Berlin. Some of them were true. You should never talk about the government. If you said anything against it, you could be arrested. If you went to church, you could not have a good job. Travel was nearly impossible. There was a six year wait to buy a car, and then it would be a Trabant. They are very small and made of plastic! That is what we were told. Food was in short supply and shops were often nearly empty. Chris and I used to wonder how two halves of one city could be so different. We, in the West, had so many shops: for food, furniture, toys and bikes. We would hear our own parents grumble at the government without them being arrested.

Chris had with him, in his coat pockets, some matches and enough scraps of cardboard to make quite a fire. It was the only way we could think of to distract the guard. The plan was to do this a little way along the road behind a parked car so that it would look worse. As it turned out, we didn't need to. An army lorry – American – drew up right by the guard. The gates opened.

"Quick, the guard's hidden behind the lorry. Run!" It was Chris who grasped the moment. I chased after him and together we sneaked through the gate, squeezing between the lorry and the gatepost. Once inside, we darted behind one heap of wooden crates, panting but safe for a moment.

We each peered out from our hidden point. There seemed to be no-one about. The warehouse doors were closed. The building, certainly on this side, was windowless. In the yard were various heaps of building materials: blocks, sand, gravel, and wood. Parked against the wall were several cars and vans. We crept from our hidden point and darted behind the vehicles. So we worked our way along to the closed double doors.

"What now?" I asked and Chris replied, "We'd better wait and watch when someone comes out." That was ages. Crouching down for a long time makes your legs ache. It was agony. Eventually one door was pushed open from the inside. A man, not in any uniform, moved out, walking backward. He was talking to someone who must still be inside. Then he turned and walked to the very car we were behind. As he unlocked it and clambered in, we were able to sneak round the back.

No-one else emerged and we had no chance of looking inside while the door was open. After a whispered conference we split up. Chris crept around the cars and stopped behind the heap of sand. That meant he could see in the next time the doors opened. I stayed put, ready to slip through when Chris signalled. We did not wait long. Both doors were pegged open to allow crates to be brought through. And he waved for me to go. I had to trust him, but I was scared. I could feel the sweat breaking through. For a moment I wanted to run away, and wished we had never started such a crazy adventure.

We would get caught, be in trouble with the authorities and at home. It was bleak. Chris waved madly again. I made my decision. I stood up and walked quickly round and into the doorway. If I was going to be in trouble, better to get on with it now. Maybe the guard would let us off.

There were people inside but they seemed to be too busy at whatever they were doing. Inside was brightly lit. At one end was a colossal pile of earth and sand. Nearby was a fenced area with a rough track going downward. This had to be the entrance to the tunnel!

Chapter Thirteen

Arrest

I waited and watched until it seemed safe for me to wave to Chris. Again, I realised how stupid we were. Two boys in a radar base or tunnel entrance could never pretend to be official. One glimpse in my direction or to Chris on his way in and we would be caught. A man in overalls called. Someone was running. Luckily, they went to the caller, and so did several others. That was the moment I needed. I beckoned to Chris, and within moments he was at my side. From where we stood, tucked behind a forklift truck, we could see the descending track and the gloom of a string of light bulbs on one side.

"This is mad, it's too dangerous," he said. Those words were not encouraging. "I think we should get out now."

Somehow, though, his words spurred me on. We had managed this much, getting through the main entrance. We had some spare time before we were due back at the garage. So I suggested he wait while I ran down the ramp to look. Reluctantly he did agree, but threatened to leave if I was longer than ten minutes.

"I'll be back in less," I said. I waited until everyone was occupied. The wait was longer because a group of men emerged carrying wooden boxes. They walked through and out of the main doors. Whilst the noise was over there, I ran. From the echoing hollowness of the warehouse, the atmosphere quickly changed. It became gloomy. It was colder and felt damp. Sounds were muffled and water dripped from the metal roof lining. The string of lights disappeared into the distance. I could hear no voices, except occasionally behind me. I suppose they were the people in the warehouse. I ran on and very quickly realised that this was a very long tunnel. Later I found out that it was about five hundred metres. It was a tidy tunnel. I had expected to run through mud and water, and for the tunnel to have earth walls. I think a car could have driven along it! I stopped, out of breath. It was then that I realised how alone I was. Ahead went the lights, dimly. I looked back and realised it was the same. What had I done? I could feel the panic returning inside me. I felt sick. too, and very scared.

Then there were voices. Where were they coming from? I turned around again to look. The voices were getting louder. Which way went back to the warehouse? Both directions looked the same. In panic I ran away from the voices. I didn't get very far, because I came to a doorway. There was a metal door set into a metal wall. I tried the handle. It turned. I swung the door inward towards me. I didn't stop to close it. Now the tunnel was different. On either side were racks of electronic equipment. Bundles of wire hung from the roof and followed the lights into the darker end. Then my horror increased. There were men sitting facing the equipment. Each had earphones on. The place smelt of stale smoke and old coffee. They did not look up, and I guessed that they were intent on listening to the recorded sounds.

By me was a large metal box. It hummed. I squeezed around the back of it and ducked my head to fit below the curved roof. Crouched there, I screwed up my eyes and tried to think. I was trapped. I certainly could not go on because one of the operators was bound to see me. I couldn't go back through the steel door because of the voices I heard. They must have come from a group of people coming this way. How long had I been? Was Chris safe back at the warehouse? Was he still there? I had a feeling that everything was about to go horribly wrong.

Suddenly a man near me spoke, "Your shift is over, gentlemen. Remember to vacate your places as quietly as possible."

There was a murmuring and people were moving about. Very quickly the new group took their places and it was now their turn to listen on the earphones. Soon it became quiet, except for one voice asking each operator how they liked to have their coffee. I crept out to look.

The scene was the same. I could see rows of equipment connected with cabling. Somewhere there must be so many tape recorders. Perhaps they were back in the warehouse.

My immediate problem was what I should do. My sweating fear made me want to run back. But I had arrived here in this top secret listening chamber. Could I find something to take back to prove to Chris that I had got this far? I peered round the humming machine and saw on the opposite side a short bench littered with tools: pliers, screw drivers and soldering irons. Amongst them were small boxes with some sort of meter built in, together with wire trailing from them. Maybe they were for testing these machines. One of these would make an excellent souvenir. I looked along the row of operators. They were all occupied with their jobs. I crept out and crossed the passage.

Then, at the very moment I had reached out to pick up a meter, a bell sounded. By it flashed a red light. I have never been so frightened. Had I set off an alarm? I dropped my treasure and darted back behind the machine. Then the tunnel burst into noise. All the operators were dumping their headgear and running through the steel door. They were shouting instructions but no-one was listening.

The door slammed behind the last one, and in that desolate moment I heard the key turn in a lock.

I was shaking and could feel cold perspiration stinging my eyes. The bell went on clanging and the red light flashed brighter than all the hanging bulbs. My way out was locked and I was alone.

So many pictures flashed through my mind. First was my mum, telling me dreadful stories about the

Communists. Suppose they were coming now? I saw again the bombed house next door to ours, and the utter darkness in the cellar. And Chris back at the warehouse. Worse than all these would be my troubles when I got home.

My terrors turned to misery. I fell to the floor and screwed my eyes tight. Maybe this was all a dream. If I opened them slowly, I would find myself in my bedroom. I tried it. It didn't work.

Again there were voices, very distant and shouting. Maybe they had found Chris and now they were coming for me. My feelings were mixed between the hope of rescue and he fear of their anger.

Then came a crash, but from further along the tunnel. More voices and a door being shaken. A shout and silence. Then a violent and deafening crack. Suddenly voices and strong torchlights. And the voices were strange; no English that I could hear. One man was clearly giving orders. I heard a little bit of German but mostly a language that I had never heard before. Before I could reach the horrible realisation that it was Russian, a torch shone fully on to my face. Another shout with a reply. I was wrenched to my feet and thrust into the centre of the tunnel. A machine gun was pointing at me.

After another brief exchange of words, I was pushed along to the door through which these Russian or German soldiers had come. Two followed me. The others gradually faded into the other direction. Another sharp crack. They had shot through the lock and, having flung open the door, ran off down the tunnel in the direction of the warehouse.

One of my captors put his hand on my shoulder and said something in German. I knew it was German but I couldn't understand any of it. He came past me and smiled. The other one said something in Russian. He sounded like an enemy! We came to a ladder and I was made to climb up it. They followed. Climbing through a trap door, I found myself in a very small room with wires going in every direction. Above me was a roughly made hole and blue sky above it. The Russian soldier shouted, and a face appeared at the hole. Arms reached down. I was lifted by the German, caught up and put down on the side of a road.

There could be no doubt about it. The Russians and East Germans had found the tunnel. The English and Americans had escaped back through it to West Berlin. I was now a prisoner in East Berlin. On one side of me was the Russian soldier and on the other, and East German policeman, a member of the People's Police.

The sandwiches were made with German bread, grey in colour and with a distinctive rye flavour. I had it sometimes at home when Anna brought some along. The meat paste was tasteless and stuck to my mouth. But I was hungry and I could not complain.

I could not complain, firstly, because I spoke little German and certainly no Russian. Secondly, because I was hardly there at a tea party! They had brought me to a police barracks and the German policeman had been told to stay with me. In other words, I was a prisoner. I knew a little of what was going on because Colonel Goncharov could speak very good English.

After emerging from the tunnel, I was told to get into a large black car. I was pushed into the back seat and then trapped between my two captors. The colonel sat in the front. His questions began as soon as the car sped off along Schönefelder Chaussee.

"You are English?" he asked.

"Yes," I replied, so quietly that he had to ask again.

"Your name?"

"Hugh."

"'You' is not a name. What is your name?"

"Hugh. Hugh Edwards."

"Why were you in the tunnel?"

"I don't know."

"Was your father there?"

"No."

"Who is your father? Where does he work?"

"Mr Edwards. He works in his office."

"Where is that?"

An alarm inside me sounded. They were Russians and East Germans. They were Communists and my mum had taught me that they were enemies and not to be trusted.

Colonel Goncharov persisted, "Did he take you to the tunnel?"

"No. I was with a friend."

"Who? What is his name?"

"Chris."

Then a burst of Russian language caused the car to stop suddenly. The Russian soldier on my right opened the door and got out, slamming it behind him.

We set off again, but not before my door was locked. Somewhere, beneath my misery, I was thinking 'Maybe the soldier was told to go back and find Chris in the tunnel.' At least, even if in trouble too, he would be safe. He had stayed at the warehouse end. The soldiers and policemen had gone no further than the sign in the tunnel that declared, 'By order of the CINC GSFG, entrance to the tunnel is categorically forbidden.' This was repeated in both German and Russian. They had pulled back at that point so as to prevent a possible international outrage.

"Your father, does he go away to work?"

"Sometimes." Then I added, "To London." I didn't add that at home we had postcards from all around the world.

"What colour is his uniform?"

"He doesn't wear uniform."

"He has an office. Is it at the Olympic Stadium?"

I know I went red at this point, but I stammered, "I don't know. He goes out after breakfast in his car."

How could the colonel know where Dad works? Was he guessing? He seemed to know more than he was saying. Then it was my turn for a question. We had been travelling for quite a time and I was still alive; trapped but not hurt. "Where are you taking me?"

"We take you to a police headquarters."

"Can I go home?"

The colonel didn't reply. He turned and talked to the policeman by my side. The conversation was in German, I picked out one or two words, but not enough to understand what my fate was to be.

The car slowed down, turned across the traffic and halted at a huge pair of wooden doors. The driver blasted his horn twice, and a guard appeared by the driver's window. They had a brief conversation before the colonel barked an order in Russian. Immediately the gates were opened and we drove into a courtyard. It was full of police cars and some military vehicles.

I was taken up a flight of steps into the building opposite the gates. We walked the length of the dull grey corridor, up a flight of stairs and into an office. It smelt of stale tobacco and worse! The lino on the floor was breaking up. The only two chairs were wooden office chairs, designed, I think, to be uncomfortable. The policeman stayed with me, and the Russian colonel left. There was a silence. I looked out of the window but could only see other drab buildings.

After some moments, the policeman spoke. He knew a little English.

"Have you hunger?" he asked.

"A bit," I replied.

"What is 'a bit'?"

"I am a little hungry," I said.

"You go to school?"

"Yes."

"My school was good," he went on. I think he wanted to talk. "I had good friends at school."

Did he want to chatter in a friendly way, or was he going to try to find out more about Dad? If I could ask him the questions, then it would be safer.

"Where do you live?" I asked.

"Live? My house? I live by Alexander Platz, five minutes to walk."

"Is it a big house?"

"No. It is small, with many other people. Three on my house. Over are five and under are two."

I guessed he lived in a flat. Then he took out his wallet. He had a photo in it. It was of a girl with dark hair. His girlfriend – certainly not his mother.

"Is that your girlfriend?"

"Ja, aber nächste Woche we are together."

I looked puzzled, so he lifted his right hand and with his left indicated a ring.

"You are getting married?"

Before he could reply, the door opened and another policeman said something about a photograph.

"Come," he said to me.

Again we walked along the drab corridors until we came to a hall. There we were met by a crowd of photographers. I was made to sit on a stool while they clicked away. Once or twice they said something to me but I couldn't understand. They shrugged their shoulders. Behind them I saw a Russian soldier. He was obviously important because of all the badges on him. He stopped the session and spoke to them all. I realised that the photos would be for the newspapers, and that this soldier, Colonel Kotsyuba, was telling them about the tunnel. Again I felt sick. I wanted to get off the stool and run. But where to? If I found my way out of the building, I would still be in East Berlin. Feeling afraid and very small, I stayed. Everyone then left in a babble of excited conversation. The colonel led them off to inspect the newly discovered tunnel.

My captor led me back to the stale office. On the desk we found a tray of sandwiches and a flask of coffee. We ate in silence. I realised I was hungry, despite the paste and the grey bread and my sick fears.

The policeman, once the plate was empty, tried again to make conversation. I was feeling far from being friendly, or even from being the enemy. I was shutting myself away in misery. I was in trouble, too much of it. If they kept me, who would know where I was? If they let me go home, there would be a fearful row. What would Dad do? I couldn't find a way out of this horrible place. I wished I had never talked to Chris about the tunnel. Why didn't he tell me not to be so stupid? Why did his dad have to get the car mended in that garage?

Maybe I was asleep. This could all be a bad dream, turned into a nightmare. If I could wake myself up, I would find myself in my bed at home, with breakfast waiting for me in the kitchen. I tried, as I had in the tunnel, but it was futile. I was definitely awake. This was all real.

The policeman looked through the drawers of the desk. He took out some paper and found a pencil.

"Here," he said to me, "Look."

I think he felt sorry for me. I hoped he didn't because if he did, it would make me feel even more miserable. He picked up the pencil and drew a grid for noughts and crosses. He gave the pencil to me. But he won. He won nearly all the games that we played. Then with his broken English and lots of demonstrations, he showed me how to win. It cheered me up because now I knew that I could outwit the others in my class at school.

"Hugh," he said, except that it sounded like 'Yoo', "I make a Flugzeug." He folded the paper into an aeroplane. It flew across the room and landed directly in the wastepaper bin. I smiled, and that encouraged him. He took another sheet of paper.

"Als ich klein war, my house in West Berlin, in Charlottenburg. I have no mother; I have no father. Aber friends have me. The man makes Flugzeug."

I interrupted and translated, "Aeroplane."

"Aeroplane?" he queried. I drew a childish shape of one on the paper.

Then he took the pencil and drew a rudimentary bi-plane. "Sopwith Camel," he said.

"I have one. I have a toy Sopwith Camel." Suddenly I had a friend. We had something in common. "I found it. Me and Chris went next door and the house was bombed. We went into the cellar and I found the aeroplane." I looked at him, but I could tell that he had not understood. So I pointed to his drawing and added simply, "I have one."

"You have? You make?"

"No. I found it in a house," I explained.

He looked puzzled. Then he said, "Ihr Nahme is Yoo."

"Yes, Hugh," I corrected him.

"My name is Hans."

Then someone came into the room. I realised at that moment that I have must have been trapped in that building for hours. Hans had helped me pass the time. It was Colonel Goncharov. He spoke such good English and was very polite.

"Hugh Edwards," he said, "I am sorry you had to wait here for a long time. Come now, we will take you home."

I looked at him, wide-eyed. How could a Russian colonel take me home? How could he go into West Berlin? Whatever would Mum and Dad say? Would the black Russian car drive up to our front door?

Colonel Goncharov led me to the door. Hans seemed to be busy scribbling at the desk. I followed the colonel into the corridor. We were going toward the stairs when Hans caught me up. He touched my shoulder and slipped a folded piece of paper into my hand. I put it into my pocket without thinking.

The three of us went down to the main entrance. There they indicated that I should get into the car. This time I was in the front, but the driver was neither of my guards from earlier. They said goodbye in English, and I was on my way home, I hoped.

We sped through the streets of East Berlin. There was little traffic, and most of the cars, I noticed, were going the opposite way. The driver seemed to be in a hurry. He didn't speak at all but he muttered, and, I think, swore in Russian whenever we were held up. He used the horn a lot, and it worked. Other cars and vans quickly moved out of the way.

We pulled up alongside some drab old buildings, and, as if from nowhere, sprang four Russian soldiers. They surrounded the car and I was told to get out. They were not even polite, but cold and harsh. I was suddenly very frightened again. They were armed and I had no idea of where we were. Maybe the promise that I was going home was not true. These old buildings looked foreboding. Were we going into one of them? I was made to walk along the street. We crossed a side road, and I noticed the name: Friedrich Strasse. I knew that name and for a moment there was a glimmer of hope. Up ahead, though not far away, were several more Russian soldiers with other men in the same uniform that Hans wore. We kept walking and as we passed them, they all stared at me. I suppose they were puzzled as to why a boy should be so heavily guarded. I wasn't puzzled, but scared stiff. We came to a guard hut and stopped. After a sharp exchange of words, in Russian again, we moved on. Now the soldiers marched, two in front and one on each side of me.

Ahead, suddenly, I noticed an army vehicle, but neither Russian nor German. It was British. Coming toward us were four British military policemen. I was going home after all.

The two groups stood well apart from one another and saluted. The one by me said one word, "Go," and pushed me. I didn't walk, but I ran, and I ran straight into the arms of one of the military policemen.

"Welcome home, sonny," he said in a Scottish accent. "Don't talk now, just come with us."

We clambered into their Land Rover and very quickly left the area, coming into familiar parts of West Berlin.

At the Olympic Stadium, where Dad's office was, we were met by a group of very important looking people, mostly in uniform. Amongst them was my dad. I ran up to him and he put his arm around me. We had to go into the building, where I was asked thousands of questions. They wanted to know absolutely everything and they were all very stern. I was suddenly extremely tired and as I sat there, I pushed my hands into my pockets. There was the folded paper form Hans. I didn't tell them about that.

Dad took me back to our house in Stallupöner Allee. He didn't speak. Sometimes he is like that anyway, but this was different. It was icy. Once indoors, Mum shouted at me in anger; about wandering off with Chris, about going into the secret warehouse, about being caught and giving away secrets to the Russians. And hadn't I been told often enough that they were bad people? Communism was evil and they were all starving over there. I was told to eat my supper and go straight to bed.

The piece of paper in my pocket said simply, 'Sopwith Camel is good Flugzeug. Viel Gluck. Hans." The first time I read it was the morning after my homecoming. I woke up late to find Dad had gone to work, and Mum wanted to go shopping. I felt so tired still. I had slept almost without dreaming. Although at one time during the night, I think, I had a dream about an aeroplane in a tunnel.

Now it was a new day. I began to wonder, again, whether the day before had been a dream, turning into a nightmare. But the proof was in my pocket. The piece of paper had a message. I put it up on the shelf. The wheels on my model bi-plane held it in place.

Chapter Fourteen

Escape from the Warehouse

If I had a new friend, I would take the Red Plane from my cupboard and show it to him. I would tell him, 'It is a model of a Sopwith Camel biplane. They used them in the First World War. And the Germans used Fokker triplanes.' Of course there were other makes, too, but I had less interest in them.

And there was a very famous German pilot in that war known as the Red Baron. I liked to think that my English plane was painted red because it fought with the Red Baron. We would gaze at it standing on the table, and we would wonder about flying, what it felt like. Was it scary, and did parachutes really work?

Sometimes, by myself, I would take it down and put it next to pictures of the same type of aeroplane. I would compare details and wonder whether to make some paper badges and markings to glue onto the wings and the fuselage. I found books in the library, near the dentist, that had diagrams of most of the First World War aeroplanes. And I read the notes, copying down the names of other famous pilots. One book described an aerial dogfight between four Sopwith Camels and German Fokker triplanes. The pilots of two Sopwiths were killed. The Red Baron claimed one victory, and his accomplice the other. His name was Udet.

So I collected pictures and notes about these. I kept them in a box, hoping to get a large scrapbook soon.

One day I was trying to draw a triplane, when I heard Chris shout up the stairs. I hadn't seen him for a long time, except in school. After the awful episode in the communication tunnel, we had hardly had time together, at least not without parents about. So he came up to my room. Very quickly my attention was taken away from drawing. Chris had come wanting to talk about that day I was caught and arrested.

Telling him what happened to me in the tunnel, and afterwards, made me sweat. I could feel how scared I was on that day. He listened until I got to the point in the story where I was driven back to the border of West Berlin. Then he stopped me.

"You know I got in a mess, too?" he asked.

"Chris, we haven't really talked much since. It's never been private."

"Yeah, but I wondered which of us got into most trouble!"

"O.K.," I said, "What happened to you? I suppose you heard all the alarms going?"

"They were. At first, people didn't move. It was as though they were each frozen into models. Then suddenly they rushed about shouting. Men came running out of the tunnel, and a big door was slammed shut at the mouth. I was scared stiff. And I was stuck. I thought a bomb must have gone off in the tunnel, or even a fire started. I was scared for you, too, but mostly for myself! I wanted to get out of the warehouse and find my dad. But I didn't know what I could say to him."

"And did you get out without anyone seeing?" I asked. I found I was getting caught up in his part of the escapade. Now it was in the past, I could almost feel some pride in what we did. Dad wouldn't like that. He was so angry for days.

Anyway, I learnt that Chris had made a dash for freedom. There was so much chaotic running around that he merged into the scurrying crowd, making his way to the main doors. He broke away from a group of men in overalls, and ran. As he raced through the open door, he was violently caught up in the arms of an American soldier.

"Hey, sonny, where do you think you're going? Or better, what the hell were you doing in there?"

He held him so tightly, and he called to someone. Two more soldiers ran over, but when they saw Chris clutched so firmly, they burst out laughing.

"Man, we're here to stop the Ruskies from coming in, and you pick up a German kid! Put him down, will ya?"

The grip loosened and Chris's captor explained that he had come running out of the warehouse. He definitely was not trying to come in.

"Soldier, you must be outa your mind. There ain't no kids in there."

The solider reddened. He was angry at the challenge. Before he could respond, there came another accusation.

"Look, you were on duty guarding this outfit. If he was already in the place, then you let him in."

For a moment Chris felt the hold soften again. The soldier, it seemed, was being made a fool of. Suddenly

Chris twisted and so freed himself. He immediately ran out through the gates to the road, dodging many others who had emerged after the alarms sounded. He didn't look back but pushed past two other soldiers at the gates. He sprinted along Schonberg Weg and round the first corner.

There was nowhere to hide. The houses each had hedges and fences against the pavement. But he was desperate. He felt his lungs would explode, and his legs were turning to jelly. All he could do was to slip between a freestanding cigarette machine and the concrete wall behind it. It was no hiding place but would have to do.

After some moments, his breathing settled enough for him to listen for any shouts, or running feet, or, worse still, army vehicles. There was nothing, no sounds except his own. He waited, but still nothing. In the distance was the noise of cars and lorries moving. He suspected they were at the warehouse.

His problems were not over. He walked along the streets back to the garage to find his dad. What was he to say? How could he explain why his friend had vanished? He should have run back. He didn't because meeting his dad became his next great fear. Was he too late?

The Goliath car was still up on the ramp. Chris could see his dad looking at a magazine. Trying to control his fear, Chris pushed the door open and sat in the empty chair by the table that was piled high with old car magazines. The explanation was simple. They had been playing hide and seek in the streets, and his friend disappeared. Having searched all over the place, Chris had come back to the garage.

After another search with his dad, it was clear that his friend had indeed vanished. The garage proprietor allowed them to use the phone. Chris listened and hoped that the British Military Police would not be called. He thought the local German police would be a better bet.

Before long the Military Police did arrive: two of them in a khaki painted car. They listened to Chris's explanation, but were clearly not taking too much notice. They left saying that if the friend still did not come back, they should telephone again.

An hour dragged by. The car was mended and it was time to go home. Again the Military Police were called. This time they did not come but gave instructions that Chris and his dad should go straight to the police headquarters at the Olympic Stadium.

By this time his dad was really angry. They drove the whole way there without a word being spoken.

At the headquarters they were shown into Major Smith's office. "Mr. Parfitt. Is this your son? And you were in the Rudow district to have your car attended to?"

Before any answers could be given, or even an explanation, Major Smith continued: "I must caution you, Mr. Parfitt, that what I am about to tell you, must, and I do underline the word 'must', remain absolutely confidential. You are to tell no-one."

"I understand," replied Chris's dad, looking most perplexed. Chris could feel panic rising. This military policeman knows, he thought. Now we are in awful trouble.

"Near where you were earlier on, there is an American forces depot. There has been some very sensitive international testing carried out. You may have seen the radar scanners on the roof. This afternoon there has been an incident there, involving a dispute with the Russians." Major Smith was not saying much, yet clearly knew far more. "We have a report of a boy being involved in this affair. We do not yet know his identity but believe he is English. He is being held by the Russians."

Chris went scarlet. He felt so dreadfully uncomfortable. He wished he could disappear, or wake to find this was a bad dream. He knew enough of the strained political situation in Berlin, to know how serious this was becoming. It was no longer a mischievous prank or a dare.

"So Christopher, suppose you tell me exactly what has been going on." Major Smith spoke firmly with hardly a note of friendliness. Chris replied quietly and explained what the two of them had planned and how he had waited behind for me to return. He told them about the alarm bells, and his own escape. All through this, neither Mr. Parfitt nor the Major spoke. Major Smith wrote sheets of notes. Then they were reminded again that they must say nothing about this international incident, only that Chris's friend was missing and would soon be found by the British Military Police.

So they drove to my home and made a poor attempt at an apology for losing me. As they were standing on the doorstep, the two military policemen, who had come to the garage, arrived. Thankfully they were able to calm the situation, and ease the increasing panic that the adults were feeling.

More than an hour later, they were drinking tea and attempting to make some conversation. It was a very strained and tense atmosphere. The military policemen were relaxed but faced the fraught father of Chris, and my mother who was fighting against total panic.

The doorbell rang. It was Major Smith. He came to say that I had been found. I had come to no harm and would be brought home later that evening. My mother broke down and cried. Chris's dad was trying to calm her. The three official visitors left. Chris sat in miserable silence, ignoring any attempt at questions, or interrogation. At least they knew I was safe, somewhere.

Chapter Fifteen

The Wedding

Hans looked across the room at Lisa. She was radiant today, he thought. He felt he must be the luckiest person alive. This day was their wedding day. Upstairs, in fact, up the stone flight of stairs in the main hall they were having the ceremony. This was the town hall, the Rathaus near Alexander Platz, and they had all their friends and families there. Below the town hall was a restaurant in the cellar. This was the place of the reception. Everyone had eaten well and the beer was flowing. The toast to Hans and Lisa had been with Sekt, a fizzy white wine. Now everyone was relaxing. It was a fine sunny April day, April 28th 1956, and warm – especially with so many guests. Cigarette smoke hung in the air and the dry smell of that merged with the tang of the innumerable bottles of beer on the tables.

Hans looked from Lisa, who was talking to her aunts. He looked down at the next table to him and caught sight of two of his fellow policemen, whom he had invited.

"Hey, Hans, how come an ugly Huferlander gets a girl like Lisa? How many sisters has she got? The two here are too young. There must be others. Why do you have the luck, my friend?" Bernhard laughed as he taunted Hans. He and Hans were often on patrol together.

Christian, the other colleague, shared a desk with both of them. He, too, teased Hans, "Come on, sit here and tell us how we find the pretty girls."

The three of them, each with a glass of beer, joked about Berlin girls. Then Bernhard changed the subject, "That stuff you did last week, Hans, what happened?" Did you really shoot the Americans in the tunnel?"

"No, no I didn't shoot them. They ran away. You know what the Americans are like; all noise and no action!" replied Hans.

"So what was going on?" By the expression on Bernhard's face, he wished he had seen the action.

"That morning, a week ago today, we had an urgent message in the office. My patrol had to meet Colonel Goncharov downstairs. You know the one; he smiles and talks politely but is cold steel underneath. He's top KGB and we were scared. We wondered what it was we had done wrong. We talked it over before we went down, but none of us could work it out."

"Yeah, I was off duty that day. If it was trouble I would have missed it," put in Bernhard.

"We went down and he told us to be at Schönefelder Chaussee, by the cemetery at one o'clock. It's the place near the border with West Berlin. You can see an American radar base not far away. We got there to find some telephone engineers digging a hole. The funny thing was there was no noise. They were working without swearing! They didn't even talk and they were using wooden spades. The colonel turned up in his black car. The briefing was that, when we were told, we had to jump down the hole and go as far as we could, with the safety catches off our guns. Rudi made a joke about shooting rats up their backsides but the colonel glared at him. It was about half past three when the engineers stepped back. We were sent down, but Captain Bartash was the first. Rather him than me, I thought. Anyway, as soon as he landed, a bell rang. It rang like a fire alarm. Then, as the rest of us jumped down, we could hear American voices yelling. There was a ladder leading even further down. We scrambled down it and dropped to the floor. Then through a steel door. What a sight there! On both sides of the tunnel were racks of electronic equipment. Whoever was in there had gone, all of them. Well, almost. We were told to search everywhere. Behind one machine I found an English boy. He was hunched up and frightened out of his wits."

"Wonderful, you all go in to catch a bunch of spies and you come out with a child!" remarked Christian.

Bernhard was restless. "That was him in the paper. We all read about it. I suppose you'll get a promotion."

They returned to their beers and changed the conversation. Hans wove his way back through the tables to find Lisa. She smiled at him and he took her hand. They came back to the 'High Table'. At this table sat Lisa's family, Heinrich and Maria, and, of course, Lisa and Hans. Heinrich asked Hans to sit with him for a moment. Lisa went to her mother.

"Hans, I have often wondered whether I should tell you a small thing," said Heinrich in a quiet voice.

'Clearly,' thought Hans, 'this is private. What can this small matter be?' Then he looked at Heinrich, "But now? Can it be important if it is so small a thing?"

Heinrich's reply intrigued him, "Yes, I believe it might be."

"Is it to be private?"

"Yes, very private." Heinrich indicated that they should leave the restaurant, but only for two minutes. They excused themselves from the family, promising to be back very soon. They came out onto the street, and breathed in the cool, crisp Berlin air.

"Hans, this is a very special day for you and for Lisa; but also for Maria and me. We are so pleased for you. Tonight you will be in your new room which will be your own home. Once, if things had been different, you and Lisa would have had a proper flat, or even a house."

"You mean if my parents were alive, and if the Russians were not here."

"Hans, be very careful with what you say about the Russians. So far our family, which includes you, and Lisa's family are safe. Do not, please, bring any unhappiness."

"Sorry, Uncle."

But Heinrich only smiled. Then he continued. "That day when we told you of your mother and father, you remember? I made for you the model Sopwith Camel biplane. It has a little clock."

"Uncle, that will always be by our bed."

"I must tell you of another. But you must not tell anyone what I am about to say. Keep it in your head, and perhaps one day…"

Hans was puzzled and felt desperately impatient to hear what Heinrich would reveal.

"Your father kept the best and most successful jewellers and goldsmith shop in Berlin. Rich and famous people came for him for rings, and for watches, for tiaras and brooches. He was a friend to them. He would employ only the finest craftsmen to make the best. Then came the terrible period when hatred of the Jews was encouraged. Your father was a wise man. He felt fearful of the future. When times became really bad, he took all his stock from the shop and hid them in a secure place. At that time, you must understand, we did not know that such destruction was imminent. He gave me the plan and notes showing the hiding place. It was a dangerous document to have in my possession. If found, it would fall into someone else's hands. Do you understand? At that time, I had several model aeroplanes, each of which was very accurate. I made them from scratch. But one was a favourite. I read a lot about the Red Baron, a very famous pilot of the Great War. His real name was Baron von Richthofen. He was flying one day with Lieutenant Udet, a younger man…"

"But, Uncle, what has this to do with my wedding?" interrupted Hans, "We told everyone that we would be only two minutes."

"Another minute and we will go back." said Heinrich with a hint of conspiracy in his eyes.

"Two things I will tell you, Hans. First, when we lived in 13 Stallupöner Allee, that house once belonged to Colonel Udet. He was promoted after that dreadful war. Second, the Sopwith Camel which I made was modelled on one which was shot down in a battle involving both the Red Baron and Lieutenant Udet. That was his rank at that time. I painted it red from the colour of the Red Baron's Fokker triplane. I used that model in which to hide the information from your father – rolled up in the fuselage."

"But, Uncle, that house was bombed. I still remember that horrible day."

"Hans, that particular model I put in the cellar. I felt it would be safer from theft or worse. I believe I was right. The cellar was not badly damaged, I think."

Hans was shaking. He felt another world opening. Could this be true? If the aeroplane was in the cellar, it would still be there. And the plan, showing where a fortune in gold and jewellery was hidden – could that have survived?

They returned to the wedding party. Lisa saw a strange expression in Hans' face, and he seemed to be smiling all the time.

That night he whispered the secret to Lisa, as he put his own model with the clock face, by their bed.

Chapter Sixteen

The Wall

For the first months Hans and Lisa were so very happy. Their flat was one room with a tiny kitchen. The bathroom was shared with others whose flats opened onto the same landing. They had been most fortunate to find somewhere to live. East Berlin was slow to rebuild after the war, and there were still hundreds, probably thousands, of bomb-damaged houses and tenement blocks. In some districts concrete boxes were appearing. Each one contained forty or fifty flats. But the waiting lists, so they were told, were too long for a young couple to be allocated one.

One day, only short time before the wedding. Hans was called into his commanding officer's room. Needless to say, that was an anxious moment. He rapidly thought back over his recent duties: patrolling an area of the city, making arrests under his superior officer's orders, and writing report after report. He, and his colleagues in the police force, were even encouraged to write about each other, noting down anything suspicious in their behaviour or amongst their friends and families. Hans would not do that and, strangely he thought, that caused him difficult moments. More than once he had been challenged and the suggestion made that he should watch his companions ever more closely.

So he knocked at the officer's door, braced himself; and when called in, marched in and saluted.

"Sit down," he was told.

"Sir," he replied.

"It has been brought to my attention that..." began the officer. This is it, thought Hans, something is wrong.

"You are getting married soon?"

"Yes, sir."

"There are questions about your reports," he continued. Hans gulped but said nothing. "Apart from that, you are a good policeman and your men respect you."

"Thank you, sir."

"I have a friend in the housing department and last night we were drinking together. As a result of our conversation, he telephoned me this morning. There is a flat free. It is not new, and it is very small. You and your woman may have it."

"Sir, thank you."

"It is at Anklamer Strasse 6. You will find it is not too far from where you are now."

Hans was lost in amazement. How could this happen, when he knew of so many people who seemed to be on lists for years? They had to apply for a flat. They had to wait years for a car. And everyone was suspicious of anyone who had a flat or a car without the endless form filling, enquiries, interviews and then the almost futile wait.

Suddenly the officer was speaking again, "Of course you will accept this offer of accommodation. It has taken a great deal of diplomacy and tact to acquire the offer."

"Yes, sir, I am most grateful to you. Please accept it on my behalf."

Privately, Hans was wondering though how many beers and Schnapps it had taken the previous night for the offer to be made. He thanked the officer, and took a note of the housing manager's name and address. He ran back down the corridor, and skipped down the stairs. Then, so as not to cause suspicion, he caught his breath and opened the mess room door slowly.

"So Hans, you are in trouble upstairs?" shouted Bernhard.

"Oh, only routine enquiries," replied Hans, but not without smiling.

Hans and Lisa made their flat comfortable and homely. They liked to have friends round, whenever Hans was off duty. They would brew coffee and enjoy sharing jokes about the struggle to make ends meet. Few references to the government were made in any conversation. Overt criticism was rare – but it was commonly understood. To make a statement against the Communist regime was to risk arrest.

They would also walk through the streets to meet others at the café by the water tower. It had continued to be the place where conversation was easier. Hans knew that it was frequented by dissenters – those who were anti-Communist and anti-government. He also knew that as a People's Policeman, he should not use the place. But he justified it to himself by saying it was full of fond memories. He and Lisa had spent so much time there before they were married.

One Friday in August, he had arranged to meet Lisa there. She had the day free from her work in the radio factory. It was the middle of the afternoon, and usually most tables would be full. Today the café was empty, almost. An elderly man sat reading a paper, and smoking a cigar. The atmosphere had changed. Lisa sensed that something was wrong.

"Hans, something has happened here. I don't like it." she commented as they peered through the windows.

"It is different," Hans spoke quietly.

They pushed open the door and noticed that the proprietor did not even look up.

"Guten Tag," Hans spoke the greeting to both the proprietor and the only customer.

"It is not a good day," replied Herr Meitzen, as he wiped his wet hands from washing up. "My good friends, I would like you to have coffee, but let me give you a little advice."

Hand and Lisa waited, and wondered what this could be.

"Go and drink coffee somewhere else. There have been arrests here, and the police may return."

"But," began Hans. "We always come here."

Lisa took his hand and they turned to leave. They walked over to the tower and into the small park. The incident in the café had cast a shadow over their day.

She had something to tell Hans, something that would change their lives. She was sure that she was going to have a baby. She had waited all day to tell him. She had imagined sitting by the window, drinking their coffee and sharing a cake. She would tell him quietly.

But now they were walking through the park, and Hans was talking about the changing mood in the city.

"There was talk in the mess today, Lisa. We have to do extra duty and it begins tonight. We were all given the orders after our patrols came in. We were late, and so the others were full of the talk. They think we will have to be by the border with the West."

Lisa said, "That's funny because at work the other day, there was gossip about new rules coming. The supervisor said that soon no-one at all will be allowed to pass between the East and the West. There was grumbling. Frank told us about the shops in the West. They are bright and colourful and full of everything to buy. Here we queue for our bread. If we buy other food, we can only have what the shop happens to have that day. Our toy shops are nearly empty; clothes shops are so shabby."

Lisa paused there, as they came to a seat. "Hans, let's sit here for a minute."

They sat looking over to the trees and the darkening sky.

"I have some news for us," she continued. Hans took no notice. His thoughts had raced on from Lisa's remark about the border being closed completely. If that were true, then any hope of him going to the bombed house in Stallupöner Allee would be dashed. Often he and Lisa had discussed how they would get there. Although being a member of the Volks Polizei, brought some privileges, easy travel into West Berlin was not one of them. In fact, it was almost the opposite.

They both clung to the hope of finding the red plane. To travel now would be highly risky. If they were stopped, his police pass would cause severe difficulty for him. They had decided that the division in the city could not possibly go on. Surely the Russians and the Allies would make some arrangement for freer travel? When that starts, they would both go to the bombed house and hope to find something of the cellar left. They were always conscious of the possibility that the house might have been rebuilt by someone. Who owned it now? Heinrich owned it before the divisions in the city. He still had the papers, but these were worthless at the moment.

When travel becomes easier, he thought, they would go and explore with hope in their hearts.

"Hans, I am talking to you." Lisa could see that Hans was away with his thoughts.

He looked at her and explained, "I was thinking of the red plane in the cellar. If the border shuts, we cannot go to find it."

"I have news for us," repeated Lisa. "Listen now." She was almost exasperated. This moment of sharing the news should be so very happy.

"Lisa, I am all ears!" Hans was grinning at her. "I am sorry."

"Look at me, look." She paused, watching his expression. "We are going to have a baby."

"We're what?"

"I think we are having a baby."

Silence.

Hans stared at her, then shook himself. "That is wonderful. Oh Lisa, that is wonderful. Is it a boy? Is it a girl? What shall we call it?" He took her hand and drew her up till they were standing together. He hugged her, and she cried.

Back at the flat they had only a short time to eat supper. Their talk was entirely 'baby talk'. Then Hans had to change into his uniform and leave for his extra duty.

At the headquarters, there was a high-ranking officer from the Russian army addressing the hall full of policemen. Each patrol was grouped together.

"You who serve the State are to be at the forefront of our new attempt to create greater freedom. Many of you have already been told that extra duties are required of you. Tonight these begin. Each patrol will be given road junctions and open spaces to guard. These are all where East Berlin meets the West. You are to seal off the area and allow no-one to pass in either direction. Gentlemen, I mean no-one. If anyone attempts to cross, you will be armed. Do I make myself clear?"

No-one even murmured.

"Lieutenant Kawolski here will give each patrol a packet of clear instructions. You are to be in place by eleven o'clock. Workmen will arrive to make a barrier of barbed wire. There will be no more talk of the West. Our revolutionary methods are superior and you, together with the USSR, will have a glorious future. Let no foolish talk spoil that for any single one of you, or your families. You may go."

The officer left with his retinue of juniors. Immediately the hall erupted into excited conversation. Hans had noted the threat in the orders. To disobey, even to complain, could have serious repercussions for families. So he found himself part of a plan to prevent any movement to the West. He was, he supposed, blocking his own way to the red plane. There had been no mention of extra rates of pay, no mention of how long these new duties would last. He felt resentful. It caused him to wonder, once again, why he had stayed on in the police. He had told Lisa it was a good job. It was steady and secure and carried a few privileges. After all, they were almost given the flat.

And yet, he suspected more than ever, he was caught up in a system that could not be right. He had carried a gun before – often, in fact. But it had been for his protection, particularly in making a difficult arrest. On one level, he had always assumed that those he was sent to arrest had broken the law. Yet something deep within him caused him to doubt. And now he was to shoot an ordinary person who wanted to go from the East to West, or West to East.

He met with his patrol, and together they studied their orders. By eleven o'clock they were to be at the Brandenburg Gate, and together with the others were to form an armed line right the way across. They were to allow the workmen putting up the wire barriers any access they required.

The others were not pleased. Many of them had plans that night: girlfriends, beer-drinking or film-watching. They did grumble and Hans had to prevent it from getting out of hand. He would be held responsible for any difficulties in his patrol.

Any official talk of building a barrier right through this city in order to create a better world for the East Berliners was not believed. Even those who had not been to the West had heard stories of the bright lights, and increasing wealth. Of course, stories are exaggerated – but there were enough tales, and there must be some truth in them.

On Saturday August 12th 1961, fifty thousand armed soldiers and police closed off East Berlin. The government was painfully conscious of how many thousands of workers, craftsmen, farmers, teachers, and lawyers had left for the West. The estimate was one hundred and fifty thousand. It was causing major problems for the Communist government.

As these 50,000 soldiers and policemen stood guard, the city was barricaded with barbed wire across its whole length. So much wire was used that it could have circled the whole world!

Hans's extra duties lasted for a short time. He returned to his normal job in the Vopos. It was the Border Brigade Guards, in grey uniforms, that manned the barricades both day and night.

As if the wire was inefficient, it was rapidly replaced with a concrete wall. Yet only two months earlier, on June 15th. President Walter Ulbricht of East Germany had declared, "Nobody had the intention of building a wall. The builders and labourers of our capital are principally engaged in housing schemes and their working power is completely employed for that purpose."

By the middle of September, those builders and labourers had already built three kilometres of the concrete wall. Most of the houses close by on the eastern side were demolished to give the guards better visibility. One hundred and thirty observation towers were built, and where the boundary ran through the river or canal, these were fenced also with barbed wire. Within five years there was a wall twenty-five kilometres long. Each half of the city was isolated from the other. Moreover, West Berlin was further isolated from the Allies, as the whole city was within East Germany.

As soon as any barriers were erected, many East Berliners risked their lives trying to get through to the West. There remained some official control points, where those with special permission and the right papers would be able to pass for a visit. It was not offered to East Berliners themselves! The famous crossing point was Checkpoint Charlie and it cut across Friedrich Strasse. Near there is a street called Peter Fechter Strasse, in memory of an eighteen-year-old who was shot by a guard. He had been trying to get over the wall. He fell and was left to die from his wounds.

Innumerable attempts were made to get into the West. People were driven by the dream of better work, and a life without fear. Some jumped from tall buildings and were caught with a safety sheet held taut by friends. Some drove recklessly through the official crossing points. These were stopped by the placing of extra concrete blocks. Some hid in lorries. One hid inside the centre of a huge drum of cable.

Stories of escape spread through the city. Names were not passed on for fear of other family members being arrested. No-one talked of plans for the next escape. You could never tell who might hear. There would be a reward for telling the police about anything suspicious.

Almost no-one talked of plans – only those small groups were desperate to make an attempt. Heinrich knew of one such group.

Chapter Seventeen

Nils is born

Hans and Lisa lived not far from Heinrich and Maria. Sometimes they would meet together on a Sunday afternoon. Walking along and gazing into shop windows would never take long. There were so few shops now. They knew also that the best articles were displayed in the windows, and they were rarely moved. Clothes looked drab, furniture was poor quality, and other things to make homes comfortable were dull and barely functional. China and porcelain were available in colourful and attractive designs, but so expensive.

The four of them would walk through Alexander Platz and along Unter der Linden. They had a favourite café nearby – favourite because of the delicious cream cakes and gateaux.

Hans and Lisa had not been to their own café near the water tower for a very long time. It had become a dangerous place in which to be seen. Every so often there had been arrests – not at the café, but in the night. The locals suspected they knew which customer was passing on information to the police.

Hans was less involved with that side of policing, and he was so glad. Making arrests of apparently innocent people made him feel sick. He felt that the crimes they had been accused of were fabricated, made up as an excuse.

There was a growing force of fear and terror. That was caused by the Stasi, the Communist secret police. The numbers of arrests, and even of people disappearing, increased over the weeks and months. At least for Hans, it meant that his duties were fairly routine. He and his companions were sometimes ordered to undertake extra duties, but by doing them well, there could be some reward. Occasionally there would be a handout of coffee beans, fresh and ready to grind. That would be a rare privilege. Two or three times there were bottles of brandy – not the best quality, but welcome all the same.

The waiter brought out a tray containing a jug of coffee, or at least, a coffee tasting liquid, and a plate of cakes. These were always so tasty. They would have apple or cherries on them, and large dollops of fresh cream.

The four of them turned their attention from the talk of the baby that Lisa was expecting. The walk to the café had tired her and she was glad to sit down. Their table was by the window, and, as they ate they watched other strollers go by. Sometimes they, too, would be looked at with longing. The sight of the four devouring cream cakes must be an attraction for yet more to come into this popular café.

After a while, when he had left nothing on his plate, Heinrich sat back and sighed. Looking at Lisa, he began a careful conversation. As he did so, he turned to see who was sitting near to them. In cafés this had become normal practice. There was always the fear of being overheard, or worse still, misheard, and the nature of the conversation being passed to the Stasi.

"You are an only child, Hans. Tell me, will your new baby be an only child, too?" he asked.

Lisa was embarrassed and looked down at her growing size.

"It depends," Hans replied. "It depends on whether we could find a bigger flat to live in. We will manage when there are three of us, but more would be very difficult."

"Doesn't it all depend on anything else?" Heinrich was obviously hinting at something more than the size of their flat.

Hans added, "These are difficult days, I suppose, and we have talked a lot about how fair it is to bring a child into the world. I know my pay is better than many others, but Lisa has stopped working. After paying the rent and for electricity, the coal, and food, there is little left."

Heinrich still tried to steer their talk away from the domestic issues of managing their money and flat. "We live in a turbulent world," he said, "There is so much uncertainty that we feel here in Berlin. Our papers tell us, almost every day, of the aggressive Western nations. It is the Americans that seem so provocative. They are the war-makers. They are developing ghastly missiles that will destroy a city totally."

Lisa responded in a way that surprised Heinrich. "We forget, here in this warm café, that we are fed not only with wonderful apple cake, or almond tarts, but with our newspapers and wireless." She lowered her voice and carried on, "The other night when Hans was on duty, I couldn't sleep. I turned on the wireless and fiddled with the tuning dial. Our programmes were all political or full of military music. I wanted something else. I found a station called 'Radio Free Europe'. Mostly it was in English, I think. They spoke too quickly for me to understand. But then a programme started in our language. It was about fashions and clothes. After that, came the news, again in German. And it was so different."

Maria raised her hand enough for Lisa to pause. Then she turned to Heinrich and suggested that he pay the bill. They would wait for him outside.

Once outside she explained, "I'm sorry, Lisa, to stop your thoughts there, but I was afraid of what you might go on to say. If we walk together now it will be alright. No-one will hear us."

"I cannot walk home." Lisa sighed. "I am too tired."

Heinrich came out and joined them, and together they walked to the nearest tram stop. Once there Lisa continued, "The news was so different. It was about President Kennedy wanting Berlin to be free. It was about the Americans trying to send someone up into space. It was about everything we never hear about. They didn't say anything about meeting our national productivity targets, or about the five-year plans we get from Moscow every day. It didn't say anything about the shortage of flour or waiting lists for our stupid Trabant cars. It's a different world. It is free, and there is colour and fun. It is so drab here. The shops never have what you need. The new blocks of flats look like piles of shoe boxes. Nobody here smiles. We each look over our shoulders day by day to see who is watching us, who is listening to our conversation. If that is what you are asking about, Heinrich, in Schmidt's back there, then the answer is no, one child is enough. We can give happiness and love to him or her. We can find treats on Sundays, and we can teach our baby to love and to laugh. But it will be difficult to teach him not to trust anyone. I hate that, I hate it."

The outburst from Lisa shook them all. She was speaking what they each knew. They, too, had heard wireless programmes broadcast from the West. Usually, these were jammed with electronic interference to prevent anyone listening. But sometimes it was possible.

They, too, had learned not to trust, which they hated. Their society, life in East Berlin and East Germany, offered some good things, but freedom to speak was not one of them.

The tram screeched its way around the corner and came toward them with its lights breaking up the gloom.

"There are rumours of escape," Heinrich said quietly. "We are told that our glorious wall dividing our city into two is to prevent those in West Berlin fleeing to the East and beyond. The truth is that it is to stop us escaping from our drab and grey lives to something with the colour and hope that you have described. There are groups of people planning their ways of getting through. Some manage it, some are caught. When they are caught, they go to prison with anyone the Stasi thinks might have helped them. As for me – I would try, too, to go to the other side of the wall."

He looked at each of them, as if to challenge them.

This was the winter of 1962. Not many days after their visit to Schmidt's café, the weather turned so cold that there was no longer any pleasure in walking through the city. Those who did, on their way to work or to the shops, looked like frozen puppets with pinched faces. Collars were turned up, and hats pulled low.

Then the snow came and most of the traffic stopped. The points on the tramlines froze, forcing the drivers to get out of their cabs with crowbars and hammers. They hammered at the pieces of rails to get them to shift, allowing the tram to keep to its route. Pipes froze and burst. Coal was rationed and so houses and flats offered little warmth.

By April the temperature rose a little. The snow, now hard packed and grey with city dirt, began to melt. Hans and Lisa dared to hope that spring was coming. As the days became longer, Lisa counted them off, waiting for their baby to arrive. She was tired, and moving about much was so uncomfortable.

Then, not long after Hans had come in from doing some overtime, he found Lisa at the kitchen table. She was obviously not right, he thought. She was panting and seemed short of breath. He threw down his hat and as he took off his uniform grey coat, went to her. Before he could say anything, or even kiss her, she looked up and smiled through her pain and discomfort.

"Hans, I think the baby is coming." So in the night, with the help of Maria and a neighbour, Nils was born — a boy looking wrinkled like a walnut. He cried as he took his first breath. And Hans, who had been banished to the kitchen, burst in at the sound, to see his son held by Lisa. The other two women cleared up and made her comfortable. Hans took up their son, and as he held him, he, too, cried with joy.

Chapter Eighteen

A Plan to Escape to the West

Hans dared to think of a new life for his family in the West. Perhaps they could settle in West Berlin, or move somewhere in West Germany. He dared to think of how they might get over or through or under the wall. He realised, too, with some despair, that it was becoming harder to escape. There was an abundance of stories of escapes – some successful and others less so.

Where the wall had been built of blocks of stones, they were being replaced with concrete. The top was rounded to prevent anyone from being able to grip there in any attempt to climb. Then, the following year, guard dogs appeared on the East side. These were loose on long chains and had been trained to attack anyone who came near them. That included the soldiers and officers. So the wall was guarded night and day by men with automatic weapons, and with these dogs. There were sections that were constantly lit with flood lighting. These drastic measures gave the area around the wall a chilling feel. Everyone shunned it, and felt fearful if they did go anywhere near.

At the police headquarters, Hans heard of a bus that had been used in an escape attempt. The plan had been to drive it as fast as possible into the gates at one crossing point. It was full of refugees desperate to get through.

Many had friends and relatives in the West. Needless to say, the bus was fired at by the guards. It was riddled with bullet holes, and became wedged tightly between the concrete sides of the guarded gate. No-one got through, and many of the would-be escapees were badly wounded. All of them went to prison.

Hans felt despondent on hearing this news. He sat during his lunch break, thinking about the futility of it all. This once proud city was split. And last year each part had been visited by a prominent political leader.

From Moscow, Prime Minister Khrushchev had come to the barrier at Checkpoint Charlie. Hans noticed in the papers what a triumphant expression this man had on his face. He noticed, too, that the people around him in the photos all looked so grey. It was the expressions on their faces.

Then at the end of June in that year, President Kennedy from the United States had come to the West side. A lot of people in the East had heard the tremendous cheering that day. This American seemed to be a popular man. There was a story that he heard about the President's attempts to speak German: he had announced at the end of his speech, "Ich bin ein Berliner." In German, 'ein Berliner' is actually a doughnut. Nevertheless, his visit brought hope to the West Berliners, and, strangely, to the East Berliners as well.

When Hans arrived home that evening, he found little Nils full of fun and mischief. He was now nearly two, and half. He could walk and run. He was beginning to string words together, some of which he must have made up. On the nights when his new teeth were coming, he would cry endlessly. They were bad times. Hans was generally exhausted from work. Lisa had Nils with her all day, often within the confines of their flat. It made the atmosphere in their home tense and snappy.

On other days there would be fun. Lisa enjoyed taking Nils out. He was fascinated, and a little frightened by the trams. Lisa gave names to them and told him stories about their adventures on the rails. Then they would go to the park by the water tower so Nils could run about and chase the pigeons. Maria sometimes met them there, or they would meet at one another's homes. Despite the grey wall and the atmosphere of mistrust in the city, they were able to have some happy times.

That June evening, Hans, tossed his cap onto the kitchen table, as he always did. Nils laughed and reached up for it. As he nearly caught hold of it, he slipped over backward. He screamed. Hans picked him up and held him close until he quietened and wriggled to get down again.

Lisa, as she made their supper, told Hans that Heinrich wanted to meet him that evening. He was to wait at the tram stop at eight o'clock. Hans was puzzled. Why didn't Heinrich come round? Or why shouldn't he go to Huferlander Strasse?

They met at the tram stop but walked on from there. Heinrich was excited and nervous. Hans could feel it by the way they shook hands, and his eagerness to walk quickly. They reached Alexander Platz and crossed it diagonally without noticing anything except who was walking near them.

Hans asked what the matter was. Heinrich burst out with the reply, "You must listen to what I say. And we must never talk about it anywhere else,"

Hans wondered for one awful moment whether something had gone very wrong. Before he could think any further, Heinrich continued, "There is a group I have come across. They are part of a plan to dig a tunnel under the Wall."

"That would be madness." Hans couldn't help interrupting. "A group of people is a weakness. Already you know of it. And now I do. How do they know the Stasi aren't in the group?"

"Hear me first, Hans. Then you can decide."

'Decide what?' Hans wondered.

Heinrich would not give Hans absolute details. He mentioned no-one's name, and gave no indication as to where the tunnel would be dug. The idea, he said, came from a West Berliner who had the rest of his family on this side of the Wall. He was determined to get them through. Because it was for his own family, the whole idea of a tunnel would have to be safe. After it was complete, a group of escapees could go through each night. Then came another shock for Hans.

"I am joining the group, Hans. Maria is, too. There is room for four more, we think."

Hans stopped, and turned to face Heinrich. "This is crazy. It is far too dangerous. Think of it: the tunnel might collapse; the Stasi could already know of it. Someone might tell someone, and so on. You cannot be serious, Heinrich. And you cannot take Maria. What if it goes wrong?"

"What if it goes right?" responded Heinrich. "We begin a new life in West Berlin. And who knows, we might find...

"Stop. Please stop and let me think for a minute."

They walked on slowly and in silence. In his heart, Hans felt a surge of hope and excitement. He knew Heinrich was about to mention the red plane, crushed somewhere in the rubble of the bombed house in Charlottenburg. He could see a way out of their plight. If it was true about freedom in the West, and a better standard of living, and freedom to follow faith: whether Christian or Jewish or something else, then perhaps the risk was worth it.

If it all went wrong, the outlook would be dreadful. Everyone would be given prison sentences. They would be split up and have to endure appalling conditions in different prisons. Whatever would become of little Nils? So far, he was happy and retaining his childhood innocence of the tyranny under which they all lived. But if he turned down this opportunity, this invitation, what then?

"I will talk to Lisa. And then I will let you know."

"No. You must not. No-one else must know. I'm sorry, I know you and Lisa tell everything to each other. In this matter you must not. No-one must know. Secondly, I have to meet someone tonight. I have to have your decision now."

He waited for the answer. Again Hans stopped walking and appeared to be looking into a shop window. His predicament was almost unbearable. If he said yes, he could not tell Lisa, maybe until the night of the escape. The risk was enormous. If he said no, and Heinrich together with Maria, got through, he would regret the decision always.

Quietly he said, "We will come."

The tunnel was dug from the West side of the Wall. Unbeknown to Hans, the idea came from Herr Betz. He was already experienced in helping others to reach the West. He had helped people over using a wire aerial runway. He had been involved with three other tunnels. Now he planned the most ambitious one yet.

He rented a disused bakery shop along Bernauer Strasse, telling the owner that he wanted to set up a photographic studio with the darkrooms in the cellars. He recruited thirty-six young people to help, mostly students.

Each group of tunnellers had to be based inside the shop for up to two weeks at a time. If too many came and went day by day, suspicion would arise. The guards might well notice the extra activity, as they watched over the wall with their binoculars. Neither could the tunnellers take the excavated sand and soil away from the shop. It was spread over the bakery floor. In order to avoid underground drains and cables, and danger of collapse, the tunnel was dug at a depth of twelve metres. No-one could stand up in it, but only crawl along. After a while the tunnellers complained of difficulty in breathing, as they dug onward. A crude ventilation system was devised, driven by an electric pump. As the tunnel extended eastward, a winch was installed to pull the trolley full of spoil back to the basement.

Disaster nearly struck at one point, when a sewerage pipe was cracked. Before it could leak its contents, the team devised a way of blocking it up again. In all, the tunnel took six months to complete.

On the East side, the entrance was in the backyard of a tenement block at 55 Strelitzer Strasse. This was not far from an East German and Russian guard post; it was within sight of the Wall and the "Safe area" cleared in front of it.

The tunnel was finally ready on October 3rd in 1964.

That evening Heinrich visited Hans's family. Lisa answered the door and was surprised to see him standing there. Immediately he indicated that they must not talk. He stepped into the flat and Lisa closed the door.

"What is the matter, Heinrich? We were not expecting you. Hans isn't home yet. He has to stay on late tonight."

"How long till he comes? Will he be here in half an hour? I cannot stay longer than that."

"But something is wrong," protested Lisa. "Is Maria not well? Or is something else wrong?"

"Sit down Lisa, for I have something very serious to explain. I had wanted Hans to be here. It would have been better." Very carefully Heinrich related to Lisa the story of the tunnel. As he did so, he watched her reactions. Nils was happy playing with a pile of wooden bricks on their living room floor. He was pleased to see Heinrich, but quickly settled again.

"Why do you tell me all this? You know it is dangerous to talk. And if you are telling people about this tunnel, then someone will inform the Stasi."

"I am telling you, Lisa, because tomorrow night, you, Hans and little Nils can come through the tunnel. Maria and I are committed. We know it is dangerous, but we are going."

Lisa felt the blood drain from her face. She felt as though she was plunged into a dream – not a nightmare, but hardly anything comfortable either. She protested that Hans knew nothing of this.

Gently Heinrich said, "He does know. He couldn't say anything because I forbade him to. He did not know when the tunnel would be ready. That is why I needed him to be here with you."

"But that is tomorrow night, Heinrich. I cannot pack and be ready. There would be so much to do. And what if Hans cannot come home in time. Oh Heinrich, I am suddenly so scared. You are frightening me."

"I know, I know," Heinrich spoke quietly and calmly. He was expecting her to explode with anger. "Let me tell you some important things, but only if you will come. Can you be brave enough?" He took her hand, and in the quiet that followed, Nils came through to the kitchen because he sensed the sudden change in mood. He sensed some fear in the air, though he could not understand. He climbed up onto Lisa's knee.

"Then tell me," said Lisa, sighing deeply. Suddenly she realised that her world would be turned upside down. Her days in the flat, the familiar streets and shops, her friendly neighbours and the grumbly old man upstairs would all be gone. She was scared for Nils, too. How big was this tunnel? How long to go through? Who would help them in the West? And anyway, how did they really know it would be a better place to live?

"Tell me about it. I am trying to be strong."

"You, Hans, and Nils, must be ready at seven o'clock tomorrow night. You must dress as though we are all going out together. That way no-one will suspect anything. After all, we have often done that. Only bring one bag, you must leave everything behind, just as though you will be returning later that evening. If you think Nils will make a noise, we will have to make a way to keep him quiet."

"But what if Hans is late tonight? What if he is on duty tomorrow? He shouldn't be, but at no notice he can be told to do extra work."

"At seven," Heinrich replied sternly, "you must leave this flat. Walk quickly to the end of the road. We will meet you there. If Hans is not home, you have to decide whether to come with Nils, or whether to lose the chance. If you and Hans are separated, he will find another way to come through the Wall."

Lisa felt stunned. Her stomach was turning over with her fears racing through her head. She couldn't do it. She just could not do it.

"It will work," added Heinrich calmly. "This is our new beginning. Who knows? You may be lucky when you go to the old place in Charlottenburg and search." He knew it was risky to use the red plane to persuade her, but he felt he must take the family, too.

"If you and Maria go, then we will come with you. I am glad I have almost no time to think about it. Hans isn't home; you must wait for him."

"In five minutes I must go to take word of your decision. Then you and Hans may talk together, but only very quietly. I have not told you everything. It is safer that way. Tomorrow is our new chapter, Lisa."

He left and only missed Hans by half an hour. When Hans came in and heard that Heinrich had come to tell them to be ready, he was shaken and angry that he had not been there. But together they planned, and prepared. They agreed that even if he was held up for any reason, she and Nils would go on anyway.

Chapter Nineteen

Under the Wall

The following day, the hours crept by painfully slowly. Hans returned to his duties after an early breakfast, expecting to be free from three o'clock. Lisa played with Nils, and later took him for a walk. She felt nervous and was constantly watching for anyone who was looking at her. Would she be arrested? Maybe it would be safer to stay in the flat. She wanted to go to Huferland Strasse and wait with Maria. Heinrich had told her she could not do that. She must have a normal day. At last, lunchtime came. For a little while she was distracted as she made hot soup for the two of them. Afterward, Nils fell asleep on her knee, and she dozed. In those moments she had uneasy dreams of dark tunnels, dripping water, and no ending.

She woke with a start. It was the dream. She thought a door had slammed, preventing her from leaving the tunnel. She looked at the clock. Hans should be home. She waited a little longer, then went out onto the landing to listen for him. Still he did not come. She went back into the flat and checked the bag they would take. In it there were only a few clothes for them, Hans's aeroplane clock, and photos of her own family. When she sat and gazed at them, she cried for fear of not seeing them again.

Time dragged by. No Hans. It got to six o'clock and Lisa was now frightened that he might not be home in time. After tea with Nils, where his appetite was as good as ever and hers was tiny, she collected up their coats and put the bag by the door. At five to seven there was still no Hans. She had to go. She was almost sick with anxiety. She scooped up Nils and covered him with warm clothes. Together they left the flat without even leaving a note, for there must be no clues left behind. Maybe they would meet Hans outside.

They met Heinrich and Maria, but they quickly separated again. Heinrich had whispered directions to her. Very soon she was knocking at the door of 55 Strelitzer Strasse. It was opened by an older man, and Lisa could see through to a courtyard. She told him their names and showed him their identity cards. He almost pulled them in, and pushed them quickly on. By a shed waited someone else – another tunneller, she supposed.

"Where is Heinrich Schmidt, and Maria?" She whispered.

"You must not talk. The child must be silent. You are the last ones because of the child. If he cries, he will make it dangerous for others."

"But my husband is not here," protested Lisa. "I cannot go without him."

"Neither can you stay," the man replied. "You are here now and you must go on."

Inside the shed it was black, but they were out of the penetrating rain.

"Now listen carefully. In a minute I will shine a light on the entrance. My friend will go first. You are to drop the child. He will catch him."

Lisa gulped and stared ahead. In the blackness, she realised, no-one would sense her terror.

The man continued, "Then you hold the pole and lower yourself down. At the bottom is the tunnel. It is low. You must crawl. Your baby will be in front. We have made a wooden sled. He will be strapped on. Don't worry, he will be frightened, but safe. We have to cover his mouth to prevent him shouting. It won't be for long. I will come after you. Do not look back. If anything happens behind you, you must go on. Do not stop, even for a moment. Just remember that your baby will be ahead of you."

"But Heinrich and Maria…"

"They have gone already."

The man shone the light. Lisa saw an open hole in the ground, where the floor of the shed would be. Before she could even gasp, Nils was taken firmly from her. She couldn't see what was happening to him. He didn't cry out, he didn't murmur. She heard shuffling and a grunt coming from the hole. A bundle was passed down, followed by one of the tunnellers.

"Now go!" the other said. She was led to the hole, where she sat on the edge. Clutching the pole that reached up to the surface, she lowered herself down. At the foot of the shaft was torchlight; and the gloomy tunnel leading into more blackness. Where was Nils? She wanted to scream. As she put her head into the tunnel, she heard a shout from above. She heard hammering and the crack of a rifle shot. A voice so close to her yelled for her to go as fast as she could crawl. Driven by the new fear of arrest, she did. She could hear further shots and a cry that seemed too close. What if it were Hans, who had been sent with his patrol to investigate?

She crawled on into the dark. She seemed to crawl forever. Her knees, she felt, were cut and bruised, as were her hands. She kept falling over her bag as she pushed it before her. There was so little air, only the stinking damp blackness. Where was Nils? Why didn't he cry out? What had happened to the tunneller behind her?

There was a pinprick of light ahead. It grew bigger. There was at last a flicker of hope. Maybe. Maybe. A voice came toward her, "Come, come quickly!"

She scrambled and crawled. Suddenly arms reached out to her and pulled her along the last bit. There were ropes hanging down. It was a makeshift winch. Someone put a loop of rope round her and she was lifted up through the shaft. Behind her were desperate voices. One was back in the tunnel.

At the head of the shaft, she was again clutched by a stranger and drawn to the edge. Her feet touched the floor of the bakery. Behind her came two more. The first was bleeding heavily. She thought it was from his arm. When the last man came up, a group of others quickly dropped huge quantities of earth down the shaft.

Lisa looked round her in a daze. Then there was a cry of a child. It was Nils, and it was Maria holding him out to her. She was so relieved, she sat down on an old crate and hugged him.

"And where is Hans?" asked Maria.

"He didn't come." Speaking these words led her to burst into tears. "I waited and waited. He never came home from work."

"Come," replied Maria. "Heinrich is in the next room."

They clambered over the piles of sand and soil, and ducked under the doorway. There, amongst more than twenty crowded together, stood Heinrich. He was covered, as they all were, with dirt and mud from the crawl through to the West.

Lisa was crying uncontrollably, so Maria took Nils back from her. Heinrich gathered them all together and said, "We are in West Berlin. We are free people. Somehow, I believe, Hans will follow. I know he will." Lisa felt sick.

That same evening, Hans was very late home. Before three o'clock he had been given orders to cover another route with his men. There had been an emergency. Yes, they assured him, he would be free to go at six o'clock. Yes, they knew he had tickets for the cinema that evening.

Then, not long before the end of his duty, another message came. He had to report to the centre in Pushkin Allee. He complained, but had no choice. Inside himself he felt panic rising. Whatever would happen? What would Lisa do? He believed that without him, she would not go. He believed that when he eventually got back to the flat, she and Nils would be there. He was wrong.

He found that he and his men were replacing another group who went to an urgent Wall incident. He was miserable and tense the whole time. He could tell no-one, and they wondered at his short temper.

At ten o'clock they were released. Exhausted and despondent he went home. It was darker than usual, with the heavy drizzle which was soaking through his greatcoat. The tram was packed with cinema-goers. He jumped off at his stop, fumbled with the key to let him into their block. He clambered the stairs, longing to see that Lisa and Nils had not gone.

The flat was empty. Then he knew. He threw of his wet clothes and fell onto the bed, closed his eyes, fighting off absolute misery.

The following day, he was due back at the headquarters at noon. He had no will to go and was oppressed with his loneliness. If Lisa and Nils had gone, then so had Heinrich and Maria. He was alone.

There was a message for him at the front desk. The duty officer told him to report to Major Kawolski immediately. He was in the third room on the right. There was no major with that name that he knew of. He knocked and went in. The look he received was hostile and foreboding.

"You are Schmidt?"

"Yes, sir."

"I am arresting you as an agent of the United States. It has been reported that you have been instrumental in trying to bring down the good standing of the DDR. You have been involved with a group of stupid dissidents."

"But I have done nothing, sir."

"It is not for me to say more. You can come freely or I will be obliged to handcuff you."

Hans was led down to the basement, and left in a cell.

Chapter Twenty

Christmas 1964

Lisa drew back the curtains. She looked round the room. It was sparsely furnished but more colourful now because she and Maria had been busy sewing. They had sewn some curtains to fit the living room window. The neighbours who had brought them also brought some bedding and cushions.

The West Berlin authorities had found the flat for the four of them. Before coming through the Wall, she had no intention of sharing living space with Heinrich and Maria. Now, with no word from Hans, she was glad for the company, and to be able to share the constant anxiety.

They had been housed in a modern flat, five floors up. Nils was fascinated by the lifts, and Lisa no longer had to climb so many flights of stairs. A neighbour told them that this block was only seven years old and had been built by a famous architect called Corbusier. Compared to her flat in Anklamer Strasse, or even Maria's in Hufeland Strasse, this was real luxury. There was a heating system that worked. The lifts worked. There were shops down below that were well stocked. It was compensation of a sort for leaving Hans behind.

Lisa had written to Hans at their old flat address. Every week she wrote again and began wondering if her letters were ever delivered. She wrote to the East Berlin City offices to find out anything. She wrote to his police headquarters. There was never a reply and none of her letters were ever returned. She was often close to despair and felt heavy with guilt that she and Nils had come through.

It was now the week before Christmas; ten weeks had gone by. She and Maria had been out shopping, trying to buy presents to put in a parcel for Hans. They had very little money, so they looked for useful things — socks and a shirt, and some chocolate, too. They took the parcel to the post and on the way back met Heinrich.

He had been to an interview. He wasn't told what it would be about, except the British people wanted to know about his work in East Berlin. He had explained that he worked for the government there on telephone networks and cable systems. They kept asking for more details until he became angry. He shouted at his interviewers that he and his family had risked their lives to come to free Berlin. He did not expect to be interrogated. The man in charge apologised and explained that they needed to check that he had been speaking the truth. How were they to know whether he as a spy for the Russians sent through this way?

They were interested in his work and would see him again sometime after Christmas. In the meantime, they hoped that he and his family would manage with the financial support given to them by the West Berlin authority.

All this he told to Maria and Lisa. They could see that he was exhausted from it. Nevertheless, he found the energy to lift up Nils and put him on his shoulders.

"Did you say about Hans?" Lisa hardly dared to hope. "Did you say we wanted to contact him?"

"I did. They listened and they wrote down a great amount. They were not pleased when I told them that he is a member of the Vopos. I explained that he tried to be a good policeman and that he was not part of the Stasi."

They fell silent, and walked through the crisp afternoon air back down to Reichsportfeld Strasse to the flat.

After tea Nils became difficult and shouted. Nothing was right for him – he seemed too distraught.

"He is tired," said Maria, "Come, let's give him a bath."

Afterward Lisa tucked him into bed and they settled for a story. Recently she had put the red plane with the clock face near to his bed. She made up stories about it and told him that the pilot was called Hans. The adventures took her mind off the real and constant fear for her husband, somewhere on the other side of the wall.

Whilst they were engrossed in the story, Maria and Heinrich made coffee and sat at the kitchen table.

"I fear for Hans," began Heinrich. "Something has gone badly wrong. We hear no word, and poor Lisa has no replies to her enquiries. We used to hear stories of arrests and…"

Maria quickly stopped him. "You mustn't say those things. Hans is a policeman; he will be safe. I think that no post goes between the two sides of Berlin. If only we had another way of contacting him."

They made Christmas as bright and cheerful as they could with anything they could adapt. Nils loved watching the paper chains grow longer, cut from old magazines or sheets of paper. Maria baked spicy biscuits and Heinrich played games with Nils. Lisa tried to put on a show of happiness. She wondered about Christmas. None of them went to church, and Lisa knew that Hans was from a Jewish family. Who, then, was this helpless baby that was celebrated with so much music and decoration?

The reality of their predicament was with Lisa, especially in the moments when she gazed at the red plane, watching the moments go by on the hands of the clock. Could there be a God who cares, she wondered? Should she pray? How should she do that? Would it bring Hans to her?

"God," she whispered, "If you are true, if you are the God of Jewish people and us, bring Hans home." As she murmured the words, she remembered the horrors faced by the Jews, and so also by Hans's own mother and father. She was not hopeful.

In the evening, as they sat talking, they heard singing. It was not from a radio, and yet nearby. There was a knock at the door.

All the neighbours on their fifth floor had gathered on the landing to sing Christmas carols. Would the Schmidt's join them? Lisa would not, and so the others left her in the flat with the door ajar so she could hear the favourites: *Holy Night, Silent Night* that the others sung every year at this time. Lisa found the melodies disturbing. They were so hopeful in a divided world and in her divided family. She lay on the bed amidst her tears and fell into a deep sleep.

The following day Heinrich insisted they all wrap up against the frost and possible snow. They left the warmth of the flat and chased down the stairs. It was a game for Nils, shouting out the number of each floor as they reached it.

They walked down their road, over Heer Strasse and came to Stallupöner Allee. Again, Heinrich wanted to see number 13, which he supposed could still belong to him. Before Christmas he had been to the city planning offices to make enquiries. He was given a bundle of forms to fill in, but given little hope.

"After all," they explained, "you left this place nearly twenty years ago. And you expect it to wait for you through the end of the war, and the blockade. You live in the East then come begging."

"I am not begging. It was my home." Heinrich came away feeling bitterness in his heart.

The trams were running, even the next day after Christmas. They waited until one ground its way past then, heading toward Kurfurstendam and the bright city centre lights. They crossed the lines and then felt the first flakes of snow fall. Once past Kranz Allee, they walked quickly to their former home. They told Nils that once there, he could play with the snow, catching the flakes and scraping more up into little snowballs.

The site looked forlorn. They had come twice before and each time the elder and the sycamore trees grew bigger. They had seeded between blocks of masonry where the stumps of the house walls remained. Their roots split them apart. Dead brambles covered the piles of debris and seemed to have sprung from everywhere, through the old floor and throughout the garden.

It was a bleak picture and curious, thought Heinrich, that it still remained a ruin. If someone else had taken up ownership, then surely there would be new building work. Maybe there was a chance for them yet.

He found a branch he could snap off. It gave him a stick strong enough to poke through the brambles, and force them back from where he guessed the cellar steps would have been. There was little to see except black ice full of rotting branches and leaves. He broke the ice and poked down through the foul-smelling mess. He could feel two steps going down. A paper plan, even rolled up tightly in the fuselage of the aeroplane could not have remained intact. Each time he had come, he still had a flicker of hope that somehow he could fulfil the wishes of Hans's father.

Perhaps they had been better off before their escape, he thought. He had come from a secure job, and a home that was small but enough for their needs. They should have stayed. It would have been better for Hans, and he could have lived with the chance of finding the red plane. Instead, he realised, the plans could have rotted to pulp. None of the three of them had jobs. They shared a flat and Nils had no father. How stupid had they all been to join the escape group. He wondered what had become of the others who came through the tunnel.

They were told that the night before their escape, twenty-eight others had managed it. They had been part of another twenty-nine. One of the tunnellers was shot in the arm and there was a suspicion that a policeman was hit by a bullet. So then, fifty-seven people had left their jobs and homes to come here. For what, he wondered? Was freedom of speech so great that it was worth losing so much?

"Come," he called to Maria and Lisa. "Let's take Nils home to tea." The snow was settling and the flakes were larger. The pavements were now slippery. They walked arm in arm with Nils skipping along by their side. None of them spoke.

Chapter Twenty-One

Prison

Hans listened to the keys. They were locking the door, and so his solitude began again. This cell was better than his last, except for the company. Before, he had shared with three others. One had been a government officer, and the others were lorry drivers. None of them were clear about any charges. They were treated like untouchable people, as though they were diseased.

When the guards brought their food, they threw abuse at the four in the cell. Amongst the swear words were others: traitor, imperialist garbage, Yankee spies, and sewer rats. When the guards had gone on, the four would carefully tell a little of themselves. They were reluctant to speak much for fear of anyone passing on further information that could be turned into accusations.

Hans learned that they each had members of their families who had attempted to break out of the East. In his case, he believed they were successful. He had heard nothing at all. He had received no letters and no information about Lisa and little Nils. If they were free together with Heinrich and Maria, then he could bear this new miserable life in this prison.

One of the others, a lorry driver, knew his family was also being held. They had hidden in his lorry on a trip along the autobahn toward West Germany. The lorry was virtually torn apart by Russian guards. They found the family cowering under a tarpaulin. The other driver said his son had organised an escape attempt which then failed. The government officer was the quietest of them all. He said little and seemed to be in the pit of depression. Sometimes he murmured about his wife. She was very ill and he had attempted to acquire some medicine and drugs from West Berlin. The person he had secretly met near to the Wall was to have handed these over in exchange for a substantial amount of money. The courier turned out to be a member of the Stasi. He was then arrested and imprisoned, separating him from his frail and sick wife.

The following month Hans was ordered to gather his belongings and follow the guard. They took him into the prison courtyard and ordered him into a black van. They locked him in the darkness. After a short time of driving over the cobbled streets, the van stopped and he was released, but only into another prison yard. He tried to work out where he was by the shortness of the journey and the type of road surface he could feel through the wheels of the van. He couldn't. He did wonder whether they had taken him around the block and brought him back to the same prison, but maybe to a different section.

They took him along the corridors, up the stairs and again along, passing other cell doors. His was number 217, and he was locked in. Here he was alone. It was bitterly cold, with trickles of condensation running down the walls. There was a concrete bench for a bed, a ledge, and a chair. On one side was a crude toilet and plastic bowl. One improvement, though, was meal times. He could meet with other prisoners at the long wooden tables. He could choose where to sit. He quickly learned who to avoid, who were the brutal bullies, and who ran black market rackets for cigarettes or other small items of comfort.

One day he was visited by someone claiming to be a lawyer who would speak for him when his case came up. He asked what his crime had been, and was told he had deserted his honourable post in the Vopos. When he protested angrily, he was told that his superior officer had written it into a report. When he asked for the date of his hearing, the lawyer had said, "Maybe next month, maybe next year. You are not considered important in the legal calendar."

Hans took a strong dislike to this man. He suspected he was some impostor. The visit ended and Hans was again left alone. So often since his arrest he had looked back and wondered. How did the authorities know about the escape? They seemed to know the people who were involved, at least Lisa and Nils, almost straight away. Someone must have passed on word.

Then in the cold nights when he rolled the blanket tightly round his thinning body, and inadequate clothes, he thought of his family, where they might be, what they might be doing.

Christmas came, but hardly any prisoners, he noticed, had any post. Christmas Eve, and the day itself was solemn. The food was no different. Certainly there was no singing, and no mood for that anyway. It was the lowest point for Hans.

He was always hungry. The icy winds found their way in through the ill-fitting window. All day he kept a blanket draped around his shoulders. For one hour he had exercise in an inner yard. It meant walking round and round, but if he found the right company, it was better than the cell.

Not long after he had been in that prison, an older man sat with him for their supper – a watery bean and bacon stew. They used the stale bread to soak up the sea of poor gravy.

The older man spoke quietly, "They came in the night and broke the door down. They said the people upstairs had tried to swim the canal over to freedom. They were shot. And I am accused of helping them and others. Who the others are, I do not know."

"I know you," said Hans. "You too are a policeman, and I have often seen you at the headquarters."

"Yes. I have been watching you since you arrived. You are not without friends."

"What does that mean?" Hans stared at him.

"Your men respected you, Hans. Yes, I know your name. They said you are always fair with them. You helped one out of trouble. I do not know what the trouble was, but it is remembered."

Hans was amazed. Here in this bitter enclosure of men, each waiting for a trial using made up charges, were words of trust and friendship. His new companion spoke one more sentence quietly, and then got up to return to his corridor and cell.

"Next week you will have a visitor, listen carefully to him."

Of course, nothing happened. Hans hardly saw his friend afterward. Each afternoon he dared to wonder. When he heard footsteps coming, his hopes rose until they went on past. So each day dragged by and his resentment grew. He began to hate the prison, the guards, and even the other inmates. He knew that was a bad sign. Maybe it was how they broke down those they regarded as dissidents. Maybe his so-called friend was planted there to unsettle him?

He hated this half of the city, with the incessant talk in the newspapers and on the radio of better times coming. Communism is the new world order, it was claimed. It gives each citizen a new freedom.

Then he found he was becoming angry toward Heinrich. After all it was Heinrich who set up the escape. It was he who caused this horrible predicament.

It was all making him edgy and moody. Six days had passed by and the only visitor had been the miserable lawyer with ever more forms and documents. It was a sham.

The following day was a Saturday. As the darkness fell together with the temperature, the guards came to release him for his habitual walk round the yard. He went with them along the dimly lit corridor. As they turned the corner, a voice shouted at him, "Return to your cell, Schmidt. The police will see you."

Hans felt sick. Could this be the Stasi? They had left him for weeks mouldering in the cold and damp. Now they would demand a confession from him. He wondered what he would have to own up to. It could be anything with those rats, he thought.

He sat on the ledge in his cell and waited. Only five minutes later his door was unlocked. Two policemen did come in but they were not Stasi. He felt sure about that.

"You may sit," said the senior one. "We are here to look at your papers. You were a policeman in the Vopos and stupidly caused trouble. Because you had a good service record, your sentence may be less severe. I have papers here, and you are to sign them. It will be easier that way. The judge will take into account your past work for the state."

He passed Hans several sheets and indicated that he should sign the top copy. As the man took them back, he slid out one sheet, folded it in three and indicated that Hans should keep it for future reference. At that point he called for the guard to let the two of them out.

After they had left, Hans swore. His hopes of any reasonable trial or a charge that had some truth in it were gone. In his hand he had a copy of this made-up accusation. He unfolded it and glanced at the yellowing paper which was covered in typescript. Then he noticed that in place of the officer's signature were the words, "Next Tuesday afternoon, be ready."

The days moved slowly on. Lost in his anxieties, he did not know how long his plight would continue; it seemed to him that he had always been in prison. Maybe those days of meeting Lisa by the water tower were only dreams. And the whispered knowledge of the hidden red plane must have been a childhood fantasy. His real world was of routine that never changed, of cold that caused every bone to ache, and of food where the taste was anything between unpleasant and foul.

Tuesday dawned, with a blizzard. He looked up at the window and saw that the world was white. The gruel served at breakfast, they called porridge. It was his group's duty that week to clear the dining hall after each meal. In a way, this was a perk. For that extra half an hour the group of them could talk as they worked. Often they would work slowly, so as to give them more time. It helped the day to pass.

After lunch, as he was swabbing the floor, he was called. "Schmidt, the police. You are making trouble for them?" yelled the guard. That guard was one of the worst. They all hated him.

Hans returned to his cell. It was the same two as before. They were very brief with him. "Collect your belongings. We have an appointment for you, an interview and a new place, maybe worse."

It sounded foreboding and yet in his mind, Hans remembered the scribbled words, "Next Tuesday afternoon, be ready." With his few bits and pieces pushed into an old bag, he was led along and down to the entrance hall. He shivered, partly from the thought of going out into the heavy snowfall, but more from fear of not knowing what would come next.

They put him in the back seat of a police car. One sat by him, with a pistol in his hand. The other drove them out through the gates and they sped away over the frozen surface of the cobbled street. They only stayed on the road because of the old ash that had been spread everywhere.

The one with the pistol replaced it in his holster. He looked at Hans, shabby in prison clothes that hung loosely off his thin body. "Hans Schmidt, you are to listen very carefully. It will help you." Then he smiled and Hans wondered what would happen next. Were these two captors Stasi or could they be friends?

"You had a message, I believe," he continued. "I hope you have the paperwork with you."

"Yes," answered Hans uncertainly.

"Reach behind you. You will find Vopos uniform. We think it will fit. We are going to Linden Strasse where there is a breach in the Wall. Yesterday there was a bomb there and several people tried to go through. Today the workmen are clearing the site ready to rebuild it. At the moment it is blocked with barbed wire. We are in Friedrich Strasse now and are stopping. I will get out. While I am out, put the uniform on very quickly. Then we go on."

Hans's mind was in a whirlwind. "What is going on?" he burst out. "Is this a trap? Am I being taken from my cell to be tricked by the Stasi?" He was very angry and fearful of being led into a situation which would incriminate him completely.

"You spoke to a Vopos man in prison? Once you helped a colleague. Now we help you. My name is Karl. This is Thomas. We do not shake hands now – that comes later if we are lucky. You want to see your wife? Then you come with us."

Hans gasped. How could this be real? The car halted and his captor got out and walked round the vehicle. Hans reached over, pulled on the uniform and tied the bootlaces as they set off again. His heart seemed to be out of control, and his thoughts raced to an idea of freedom.

It was gloomy now. More snow clouds drifted over the space. The street lights lit up empty shops and a few walkers. Two streets later he saw the breach in the wall. They stopped with the headlamps shining on to the barbed wire. Hans was ordered to get out with both of them, but to say nothing. The freezing wind whipped across their faces. Karl pulled up the collar of his coat and straightened his cap.

There seemed to be no-one else around, until out of the shadow of the Wall appeared two workmen and a guard. Karl, Hans had noticed, was the senior of the two. He moved toward the guard and workman. As he did so, he drew from his greatcoat an identity card. When the guard saw it, he quickly came to attention and saluted. Karl said he had come to inspect the damage to the Wall and the imminent repairs. He put away the stolen Stasi card and sent the guard to fetch his own superior officer. The workmen were told to move over to the pile of sand and sacks of cement. His hand went again to his pocket. He drew out a large pair of wire cutters. As he did so, he called softly to Hans and Thomas, "Get back in, start the engine and when I shout, drive here, pick me up and go on. Then stop for nothing."

It seemed to take so long to cut the rolls of barbed wire. But before the official wall guards returned, Karl had pulled back the cut lengths.

"Now!" he shouted, "Now! Now!"

Hans and Thomas, in the car, raced forward and slammed to a halt. Hans flung open the back door for Karl to jump in. As he did so, a searchlight came on and swung toward them. "Faster, faster, come on man." he yelled. Then a burst of gunfire shattered the windscreen. Thomas wrestled with the steering wheel; Hans clung to the back of the front seat. They lurched on to the junction with Oranien Strasse and stopped. Soldiers came at them, both on foot and very quickly after in an armoured car.

"Raus, raus. Get out, get out, put your hands up!" screamed the first one. His machine gun was trained on them. The three clambered out with their hands up. Hans was nearly sick, anticipating something worse than a return to prison. Where did these Russian soldiers spring from?

Then the first man lowered his gun and said in an American voice, "Welcome to West Berlin, buddies."

There were orders being shouted out, but they were through the Wall. Hans realised with a rush that prison was behind him. He, Karl, and Thomas were in the West. And somewhere was Lisa.

Chapter Twenty-Two

Reunion

Maria went to the door. It was very rare that anyone would come up the five floors and knock. There stood a man in a suit, together with a West Berlin policeman. The sight of the police or military uniform still created fear in her, even though Hans was a member of the Vopos.

"Frau Schmidt?"

"Yes," she replied warily. "What do you want?"

"I am sorry to trouble you but if I might come in, I have some information for you."

Maria measured his words. They sounded trustworthy. Maybe it would be about the bomb site that Heinrich was attempting to claim back as their own. She stepped aside and the two came into the little hallway. Nils saw them and ran to hide behind Lisa. They were led into the kitchen.

"Please sit down. I will call my husband." Maria left Heinrich to deal with the situation. She was glad to leave them to it, feeling old anxieties. Then, within moments, Heinrich called with tremendous excitement.

"Maria, Lisa, Nils come quickly."

They rushed through and squeezed by the table to see the two visitors. Heinrich continued with difficulty. He felt a lump in his throat. "This gentleman, I'm sorry I don't remember his name. He has come to tell us that Hans is safe."

No-one spoke for what seemed minutes. Then Maria burst out, "Oh thank God, thank God."

Heinrich continued, "He is safe, Lisa. He is in West Berlin now."

"What!" Lisa almost screamed, "Where? Where is he?"

Maria burst into tears. Heinrich swallowed hard, and after a moment the visitor explained, "He and two others came through the Wall. At the moment we are unable to give you any details. He has to be interviewed first thing tomorrow morning. For now, he must have medical checks and we have to verify his identify."

Lisa broke in, "I must go to him now. Where is he?"

"I'm sorry but that is not possible. You see, when anyone from the East comes through they have to be screened. We must be sure that they are genuine refugees. You four here must have been through that process. It doesn't take too long. It is very likely indeed that he will be released tomorrow lunchtime. If there is any delay, I will let you know. If not, you can expect him here."

Lisa could not sleep. Most of the night she was up, pacing round their living room. She picked up a magazine but only stared at the pictures. She tried the wireless, but did not hear the programme.

In the early hours Maria came through. Together they made coffee and sat and talked. Eventually dawn came, and the morning dragged slowly on. Heinrich went out early with Nils and returned with a packet of streamers. Nils then helped him hang them on the front door. They fixed them across to the lift doors.

By two o'clock Lisa could stand the tension no longer. She propped open the door and stood watching the lift indicator. Soon one was coming up. She held her breath. It stopped. The door slid open and there stood Hans. She ran to the lift and threw herself at him. He dropped his bag and hugged her. The door closed and they found themselves going down! They laughed, and laughed.

Later, Hans leant back in the bath. It was full of clean hot water with a bar of soap. It was luxury as he had never known it. Maria reminded him of his childhood bath times and the stories she told him at his bedside. Now he was so thin, Lisa noticed, and grimy, too. The prison showers had been cold and only occasionally tepid. Soap was scarce and could be traded with cigarettes. Now, gradually, the dirt of his prison life was washed away.

Only after a joyful meal together, with Nils clinging to him, did he tell them of his ordeal in the two prisons. He described the escape and how it seemed to happen without his planning. He said the first visitors they must have should be Karl and Thomas. Even now, he explained, he knew little about them or whether they had families.

Lisa took him to bed. The sheets were crisp and clean. The bed gave a little under his weight instead of being cold and hard. He slept.

Nils shook him awake. For some moments he thought it was the guards. His dream was of a warm and wonderful homecoming.

"Papa, Papa." Nils shook him again. The fears vanished, and he remembered. Nils climbed up and sat on him. Lisa was already up.

There was a knocking at the door of the flat. Heinrich went saying, "Only sometimes do people come. First it is the two with our wonderful news. Next it is Hans. This is the third time."

It was the postman bearing a large stiff envelope. Heinrich signed for it, thanked the postman, and brought it through to the kitchen. He took a knife and carefully slit it open, sliding out the contents. It all looked very formal and very official. There was a letter with forms and documents. Heinrich scanned it and stopped.

He read it carefully again. Maria was cutting cold sausage and cheese for their breakfast. Heinrich stood up and went to her. He put his arms round her and said, "Maria, my dear, this letter says that our house is ours."

"What did you say?"

"Our house is ours. Maria, our demolished house over in Stallupöner Allee. The city planning office has sent us the papers showing we are the true owners. If it had been rebuilt by someone else, it would have been very difficult. One day, soon, it will be our home again."

Hans came in to the smells of coffee and breakfast. Nils clung to him, clutching a toy in his other hand. He picked him up and sat him on the table between the set places. He was almost serious in thinking that this must all be a dream. Soon the reality of the prison breakfast slurry at eight o'clock would return. How could he remain in this wonderful peaceful and happy world?

Lisa was talking to him, asking so many questions that he begged her to stop. "Later I will tell you everything. Maybe today," he said, "Maybe more tomorrow. First you must show me that this is all real. We are in West Berlin? We are together anyway."

Heinrich described the letter that had come. "Today, Wednesday, we have here. Tomorrow, I have to go up the road to the Olympic Stadium. There I will have another interview. Someone from London has to see me and hear about my work for the telephone systems. Maybe I will have a new job here in the West."

"Then," said Lisa, "tomorrow Hans and Nils will come with me over Heer Strasse to number 13."

Chapter Twenty-Three

An Accident

Edinburgh House was really a hotel for British forces people staying in Berlin. It was now about three years since we had moved back to England. My father's work was in London, which meant a train journey there and back each day. I still had a few mementoes from Berlin up on a shelf. The Red Sopwith Camel was in the middle – I suppose because I came across it in such an unlikely place. Memory of my arrest in the tunnel was not happy and even now I sometimes have nightmares about it. Although I failed to find anything in the tunnel to give to my friend Chris, I did still have the folded piece of paper given to me by my guard as I sat in the East Berlin police station. Lately it had become a bookmark for when I read any book about the history of aeroplanes.

For this visit to Berlin I had brought with me a book about aerial battles over the fighting in the First World War.

It was now time to go out, so I put the book on the floor, upside down so it would stay open at the place. Today, as we were visiting where we lived and where my father was based at the Stadium, I wanted the bookmark with me for what is called 'old times' sake'.

Chris and I met my father on the landing. Our room was at the front of Edinburgh House overlooking

Theodor Heuss Platz. There was traffic all through the night, so we only slept lightly. My father was given a room at the back with no special view, but it was quiet.

He had brought us on this brief visit as a special holiday, having survived our exams in the school fifth form. It was, for him, business mixed with pleasure. Today he would drop us off at Heer Strasse so we could see where we each had lived, and walk round the back of the houses into the woods. That was where we had spent most of our free time, sledging in the winter, roaming with other friends in summer. Behind the woods was the artificial hill with its ski run, all built from the rubble of the bombed city.

He could not be with us, he explained. In the offices at the Stadium, he had to meet a German who had come from East Berlin. It was something to do with telephone engineering. It sounded boring to us!

Chris's house looked exactly as we remembered, except the front fence was wildly overgrown with weeds. He pointed to his bedroom and we talked about our planning there for ventures into the woods or down the Havel lakes.

Our house had been repainted. There was a brass plate on the front gate post. Otherwise, it looked no different. We laughed, wondering why we had even thought that our houses might have changed. Generally, they don't, we reflected. Normally houses stood for hundreds of years, or at least could do.

"Let's go back and see the ruin next door," Chris suggested, "It looked even worse just now when we came by."

It was worse. There was heavy wire mesh fencing along the front by the pavement. Inside, trees had sprouted everywhere. Brambles and the nettles were spilling through the wire. The front gate was ajar and we wondered whether to push our way in. We didn't, because we could hear voices not far away. With very little knowledge of German, we did not want to have to explain why we were snooping.

As we stood there, each remembering our venture into the cellar, there was a sudden movement. A child, not very old, slipped through the gate and ran into the road. Two cars were coming.

"Quick, quick," yelled Chris. We ran and grabbed hold of the child, taking him to the pavement on the other side. The first car screeched to a halt. The driver got out and, I think, swore at us for being so stupid with a child. The other driver blasted his horn, shouted something and drove on.

As the two cars moved off, a couple appeared through the gate. They saw the child and ran over to us. The man picked him up and became angry with us. It was a stream of German so neither of us could understand.

"I'm sorry," I blurted out. I didn't know what else to say.

"You are English?" asked the woman, "I speak a little."

The man argued with her, but she persisted. "This is our child. I think he was in the street."

"Yes," I said, "He was nearly hit by the cars."

"You made the child safe," she continued. "We must thank you."

The man spoke to her and she tried to translate. "You live here?" she asked.

"I used to. We went back to England three years ago. Now we are here for a holiday," I explained.

The man spoke again. I noticed how thin he looked and wondered when he had last had fish and chips – or in Germany, it would be sausage and chips. He looked at me closely and I felt very uncomfortable. Chris was agitated, too, I could tell.

"Your name? What are you called?" he asked. So he could speak some English.

"Hugh." I was not going to give my surname, certainly not to this stranger.

Then he tried to repeat it, "Yoo, ihre Nahme ist Yoo." He paused then added, "I think you have Flugzeug, Sopwith Camel?"

Chris gasped in surprise. Then I immediately knew him, the friendly guard after my arrest.

"Yes, yes and look." I took from my wallet my bookmark and read it to him, "Sopwith Camel is good Flugzeug. Viel Gluck, Hans."

"I am Hans," he said. "And you have the red Flugzeug?"

The woman, his wife I realised, was not listening. She had taken the little boy to comfort him after his frightening ordeal in the road. Hans continued in his broken English.

"I was small. Here is my house." He pointed to the ruin. "When I was small I have Flugzeug Camel. It is in there." He pointed and laughed realising how futile it was even to remember.

"Then," I added, "My aeroplane is yours. And you must have it back." What else could I say, when he looked so hungry and poor, as did his wife and boy? "It is in England and I will send it in the post."

Sopwith Camel